THE VIKING AND THE DRAG QUEEN

Campo Royale #1

V.L. LOCEY

The Viking and the Drag Queen

Who will emerge the victor on the battlefield of love?

Tyr Hemmingsen had his life mapped out at a young age. The only son of the late Danish hockey great, Elias Hemmingsen, Tyr has always done his best to follow the plans his father had laid out for him. Finish school, make it into the pros, become team captain, find a biddable young lady to marry, and win a championship so the Hemmingsen name lived on eternally on the side of a massive silver cup. Like the good son he is, Tyr has done as his father wished, no matter how it peeled away layers of his true self. Then, all the neatly placed supports that hold up his so-called life come crashing down during a night on the town. Tyr might be known as the "War God of Wilmington" on the ice, but there's no battling the effect Gigi Patel LeBay has on him.

Elijah McBride lives for the spotlight. As Gigi, he bewitches and bedazzles the crowds at the Campo Royale

Club. His vibrant stage persona is the face he presents to the world. Underneath the rouge, eyeliner, and lipstick is a young man who still feels the sting of his parents' disapproval and rejection of the son who wears wigs and dates other men. With his drag family and older brother in his corner, he's finally found peace in his life. Until the fateful night a massive hockey player shows up at the club. There's a world of hurt in Tyr's soft brown eyes, and Eli finds himself falling for the big man, despite all the barriers he's built around his tender heart.

Newsletter

Never miss a release

If you want to keep up with all the latest news about my upcoming M/M releases, sign up for my newsletter by visiting my website:
vllocey.com

Acknowledgments

Stick Taps
To my family who accepts me and all my foibles and
quirks. Even the plastic banana in my holster.

To my alphas, betas, editors, and proofers who work
incredibly hard to help me make my books the shiniest we
can make them.

To Rachel who helps keep me on time, in line, and
reasonably sane.

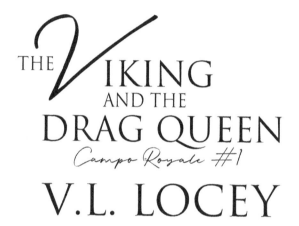

THE **VIKING** AND THE **DRAG QUEEN**

Campo Royale #1

V.L. LOCEY

Prologue

TYR

"Tell me the story of your namesake."

I glanced up from where I sat on the floor, the bed at my back. I hated to gaze upon him as he was, yet Mama insisted I not look away. I ran a finger over the threadbare carpet. 'He needs to see your face, my son,' she would say, then go hide in the garden shed, her legs tucked under her, staring at the hoes and watering cans sometimes for days. I would bring her food and water when she was in the shed. It was all I could do.

"Can I tell you one of the tales that I wrote?"

"No more talk of writing stories. Put those away. You'll play hockey…do what I failed to do. Now, tell me the story of your namesake."

"Which one, Papa?"

When Mama was caught in the darkness that stole her away, I stayed on the floor, the chair beside his bed empty. He would pet my head with a skeletal hand. It was so unlike the strong hand that used to hoist me to my feet after a tumble on the ice.

"The most heroic telling," he rasped, his fingertips buried in my overly long hair.

I sighed, wishing to be anywhere but in this sick room. All my friends, my teammates, were out playing in the snow or skating on the frozen ponds of Ribe. I was here, alone, watching my father wither away physically as my mother shriveled mentally. It was no place for a twelve-year-old boy, all the neighbors whispered.

"When the dread wolf Fenrir was a mere pup, it was quickly noted that he was growing into a massive hound, far bigger than any other. This scared the gods, so they attempted to shackle him in fetters that he would never break free from."

"And which god was willing to do so?" he asked, his voice brittle as a leaf touched by winter.

"Only Tyr was willing to do it, for he had raised Fenrir from a suckling pup. Of all the Aesir, only Tyr knew how to keep his emotions in check, for the blood of Jotenheim ran in his veins. The gods went to the dwarves and had them fashion a chain that would hold the dread wolf, as all other normal chains had failed. And so, they presented the chain, Deceiver, to the wolf, but he was not fooled. Fenrir declared that he would only allow the gods to place him into bondage if one of them would put their hand in this muzzle as a show that they would not break their oaths. Only Tyr was willing to do so, for he loved Fenrir."

"None among the Nine Worlds were more honorable than Tyr."

"Yes, Papa. And so, Tyr placed his hand into the mouth of the dread wolf, and he was bound. Tyr sacrificed his hand and his honor. Then, his power grew weaker, for he had betrayed Fenrir and his word was no longer honorable."

"Yes, yes, and tell me…" He paused to draw in a rattling breath. I squeezed my eyes tight, pulling up a vision of the man my father had been just two years ago. Robust, tall, wide as a ship, loud as a raging bull. A man every man admired. Athletic, proud, regal in his bearing. The man who had taught me to skate before I could walk properly. "Tell me what that story means to you, Tyr."

Tears ran down my cheeks as the breathing machines inflated his weak lungs. "It means that a man must never break his word to those he loves, lest his power wane. For if you break an oath, your strength will pass to the tree-hung-one and you will be forgotten."

"That is right." He scratched my head, his long, brittle nails scoring my scalp. "You must never break your word to me, Tyr. You must honor me as I have asked. You must take care of your mother…" He stopped to breath. His time was short, Mama said. I sniffed up a tear, the salt burning my nose. "You must be the man that walks in my place. Live my dream for me. Marry well. Fill up this house with children. Tend to your mother. Hold the Cup over your head. See that our name is engraved on its side. Do it for me, Tyr, for I have fallen short of my goals, but you are strong. You are the strongest of them all."

"Yes, Papa, I will do what you could not."

Chapter One

TYR

Thirteen years later

THE SPOTLIGHT WAS ON ME. I HATED PUBLIC SPEAKING, AND so I shuffled my note cards and adjusted the beret atop my head. Anything to stall. When the people at the fancy tables began to grow restless, I cleared my throat, my gaze slipping to my friends and date.

"Thank you all for coming out tonight in the cold and snow to attend the Wilmington Sports Writers Annual Dinner and Award Ceremony." I looked up as Dante had told me to. Ugh. So many people all waiting for me to say something witty. Wit wasn't what I did. That was Dante's forte. All I did was skate hard and hit harder. "I know many of you aren't fans of the cold, but for a man named after a Norse god, this is springtime." I waved at the windows that were frosted solid. The crowd laughed softly.

"As the recipient of this incredible award," I patted the ten-inch tall crystal trophy sitting on the podium with care, "I'd like to thank the Wilmington Warthogs for their amazing coaching staff and management. If not for them, I'd not be here. They were willing to take a chance on the kid from Denmark who had a so-so slap shot." That got me another round of chuckles. I had more than a so-so slap shot, but hockey players were not braggers. The NHL did *not* want glory hounds. Leave that to the football players. And I was *this* close to the pros. One more season in the AHL, everyone said. I had to walk the line, be the man that the world and my father wanted me to be.

"Thanks to my teammates for putting up with my dour moods and lack of any sense of humor." I heard Dante roaring from his seat. The rest of the crowd joined in. I smiled out at the sea of faces, happy to see that I was pleasing them. "Thank you to the fans who have supported me since I arrived here from the University of Prague—Go UK Praha!—who warmly welcomed me to the great town of Wilmington." My tie felt too tight around my throat, but Janine had said it was fine and matched my beret, so all was good. The MC of the night, standing to my left in the shadows, cleared his throat. "Before my time runs out, I must thank the sports writers of this wonderful city for choosing me as the Athlete of the Year. Thank you all very much."

Flashes from a few hundred cameras and phones blinded me.

I gave them a short bow, grabbed my award, and was led off the stage by a lovely young lady in a dark blue gown. It was quite the prestigious event, despite the less than stellar setting. The old hotel had seen better days, but journalists from all over the state of Delaware had driven through the wintery weather to attend. I shook a few hundred hands on my way from the backstage area to my table. Dante rose from his seat to hug me and slap my back when I finally rejoined my friends. Janine smiled up at me, pride in her big blue eyes. She was, by far, the prettiest woman at the table, and that said something, as most hockey girlfriends/wives were stunning. I sat down on her right, then placed the award on the table beside my empty dessert dish.

"You nailed those jokes," Dante said as he leaned around his date.

"You wrote them," I replied as the MC began wrapping up the event.

"And that's why they were so perfect." He grinned at me before kissing his girl on the cheek. I felt like I should do something similar, so I leaned over to place my arm around Janine. She snuggled in close, but I had to wonder how long it would take her to start suspecting something was off with us. We'd been dating for two months now, with only a few kisses shared. Soon, she'd begin questioning me, asking me if I found her attractive, and then we'd have to break up before she put two and two together. Which sucked, because I genuinely liked Janine. If only she would be happy with just being friends. But she wouldn't be, and I couldn't hold that against her. She was a beautiful young woman with a new nursing degree who modeled on the side. The world was full of men who would desire her sexually, as well as mentally. The end for us was predestined.

"We should do drinks somewhere to celebrate," Dante's steady girl Maya suggested. I glanced from Janine to my line mate. I played right wing, Dante played left, and centering was Ben Doyle, the man seated across from us, making out with a redhead whose name we never did get. Probably Ben didn't know. Ben went through women like most people go through socks. Being on the cusp of greatness was one hell of an aphrodisiac. Add in that he was cute as hell and had tons of charm, and who could resist him? Women flocked to athletes. A different chick every night for someone on the first line who was poised to make the leap to the pros within a year made tallying up conquests easy. Well, for Ben. Dante was more a one-woman-man, and I was…well, I was keeping a secret that would probably die with me.

Ben came up for air at the mention of drinks. He liked to party. "Hell, yeah. Tomorrow's not a mandatory skate. Let's celebrate our man Hems racking up another trophy for his case!"

His tone was cheerful, but I suspected that our star center held some kind of resentment toward me. There was no one thing or episode that made me feel that way, just a lot of small little comments and soft jabs. Or perhaps I was being overly sensitive. Despite what the fans and our local announcers thought, I did have feelings. They were just deeply buried. Like down around the core of the Earth deep.

"It *is* kind of Boomerville here," Janine threw out. We gathered our coats, I helped Janine into hers, and we left the stodgy old Wilmington Way Hotel in our dust. It was barely nine at night, so we made a sweeping tour of a few well-known nightclubs. Since it was a Wednesday, none of the hot places were really cooking. I wasn't much of a dancer, so the one dance club we stopped at made me grimace. Janine never said a thing, as we all had one drink, then left. She did sneak in a dance with Maya, which

Dante and Ben enjoyed watching. I pretended to find the two women bumping hips as hot as my friends did. I was pretty good at acting by now.

Around midnight, we were on the sidewalk outside the dance club, coats up to our ears, breath fogging in front of us. The girls were freezing, their bare legs exposed to the cold.

"So, are we calling it a night or what?" Dante asked, his arm around Maya. I held one of Janine's cold, tiny hands.

"No way. Let's see what we can find that will jazz up this loser of a night." Ben looked up from searching on his phone. "Oh sorry, Hems. Not that you're a loser. You win everything."

Ouch. I glanced at Dante. His brown eyes narrowed. So it wasn't just me. Good to know. I had no clue how to fix things, but someday soon I'd have to talk with Ben. We couldn't have bullshit like jealousy leeching into our play. We all had too much at risk.

"There's that place that my cousin works at," the redhead who had introduced herself as Brenda said. "It's a blast! Honestly. He waits tables, and says the shows are top-notch. I love going there! Although, you guys might not like it. It's a drag club."

The girls all squealed. Ben frowned so deeply the furrows on his brow made him look like a Bassett hound. I felt a chilly finger go down my spine. Weren't drag clubs just fancy names for gay bars? I'd never dared venture into a gay bar. I couldn't risk giving myself away so carelessly.

"Uhm," I said, but was rolled over by the girls and Dante stating they would love to do a drag show or two. Ben muttered about being outvoted. I smiled my best fake smile and piled into the Uber that rolled up five minutes later. It was a tight fit, but we managed to make it work.

"I could have sat on your lap," Janine whispered before her head settled on my shoulder.

"Yeah, that would have been sexy," I replied softly as my fingers meshed with hers. Conversation was light as we made our way to, what I hoped would be, our final destination. I was tired and had been hoping to make it an early night. I'd planned to attend morning skate. I never missed. You didn't make it into the pros by skipping practice.

"Here it is!" Brenda shouted, breaking the lip lock Ben and she had been sharing. "Campo Royale Club! I love it here!" She was out the door before the car was fully stopped. Damn daft woman. Ben left the driver payment and tip to Dante and me. Nothing new there.

The outside of the bar/club looked normal enough. Just a redbrick façade with a neon sign in the shape of a red pair of lips. The name of the club sat smack dab in the middle of that big flickering mouth. Music thrummed through the walls.

"If one fag touches me, I will freak out," Ben grumbled, his speech slightly slurred. The girls hissed at him. I rolled my lips over my teeth, pulled my dark blue beret down to my eyebrows, and ventured inside. Janine had my hand, so I really had no choice but to go in. Two huge bouncers just inside the door carded us as music so loud it made my fillings throb blared out into the small hallway. We pushed through swinging doors after paying the cover fee and that was when my feet decided to stop moving. The club was dark, kind of cavernous feeling, with a long bar on one wall, tables packed in mish-mosh—all of them full—

and a big stage at the back of the room. There was a woman—no, a man, it had to be—on stage in a cowgirl outfit singing—no, lip syncing—to some old song about buttons and bows. My mouth hung open as my eyes adjusted. There were queer couples everywhere. Ben gave me a shoulder bump.

My gaze flew from a gay couple at the closest table who were sitting side by side facing the stage, clapping and singing along. They had to be at least sixty if they were a day.

"Do you know what they call old fairies?" Ben shouted over the drag queen currently on stage with her toy six-shooters. "Faggies."

"Dude, really?" Dante spat as the old gay couple turned to glower at us. I felt six inches tall as opposed to six foot four. "Stop with that shit. If you can't be cool, then go the hell home. Hems and I will entertain your lady."

"Seriously," Brenda sniffed, then stomped off toward the bar with the other girls.

"Whatever. One drink then we're out of here," Ben snapped, shoving around me to get to his date and pull her to his side. Guess he was scared a lesbian customer would hit on Brenda. The way Ben was acting, Brenda would be much better off wrapping up the night with a pretty lady to buy her drinks and kiss her goodnight.

"Guy's a real jerk when he gets a few in him. Just ignore him," Dante shouted in my ear, then clapped my shoulder. I stared after him in confusion. Then, the lights came on and the cowgirl took her bows to wild applause. I fumbled along after my friends, my gaze moving over the crowd, then the MC, who was now sashaying onto the main stage. He was clad in a sparkly red dress with a huge blond beehive wig atop his head.

"Another big hand for Annie Oak Lee," the MC said in a deep, bored monotone that did little to inspire applause. Yet, the crowd hooted and stomped. "I love a girl with big six shooters," he commented, then patted his wig. "Next up on our theme night is one of your favorites. A tiny nightingale with a powerful voice whose pussy is on fire of late. Yes, she is part of the house of Patel, I'm proud to say. Sitka Patel only takes the best bitches under her wing."

The patrons shouted "Sitka! Sitka! Sitka!" and the much older Black man on stage bowed dramatically, his wig never moving. I wiggled into the bar behind Janine, my hand resting on her hip in what I knew was an intimate gesture of possession. She leaned her hip into my palm. A slim bartender wearing rainbow suspenders over a skinny little black crop top with the club logo appeared. His eyes were lined with purple glitter and his hair was bright pink.

"Just a Sprite, please," I called to the bartender. "This round is on me." I slid a fifty across the bar, then motioned to the others in my party. As our drinks were being made, I studied the crowd again, stunned at the amount of people who were making public displays of attention all over the place. I'd never imagined it. A place where a person could simply be who they were. What the hell must that feel like?

Wonderful. It must feel wonderful.

I quickly choked down that weak little voice that resided inside me. The MC began clapping, then bowed off the stage. The lights dimmed. A screen behind the stage began showing a video of what appeared to be a rainy Parisian street scene. Janine smiled over her shoulder at me, the soft pink lights roaming over the crowd making her look even prettier. I placed a kiss to her shoulder, then my eyes were pulled to the stage as a cold glass of soda was placed against the back of my hand. I never looked at the glass resting against my knuckles. How could I have glanced at it, when the most stunning vision I had ever seen was now taking the stage? She curtsied to the mad applause, then lowered the microphone. She looked diminutive, even from across the room, but she had such beauty and grace. A presence that held a person spellbound.

Her dress was purple. Janine and the other girls were whispering about how beautiful the lilac, off-the-shoulder, tea length, chiffon lace cocktail dress was. Oh. Okay. It was lilac. The singer's hair was the same color. It was a huge cloud of soft purple and white beads that framed her heart-shaped face. She moved with incredible elegance on pointy-toed, lilac stilettos with beaded ankle straps. Her calves were shapely, her ankle finely boned. I yearned to touch her smooth skin.

"Good evening," she said into the mic and my heart rate tripled. "My name is Gigi Patel LeBay, and I'll be entertaining you for the next hour." Her voice was manly, yes, but not overly so. She spoke softly, sensually. I could *not* look away. She smiled out at her admirers. "We're going to roll back the clock to the days when men were men and women were double-breasted." She caressed her breasts. The club goers laughed loudly. My cock began to swell. It was hard to swallow. Janine moved back into me, just a bit, her ass resting against my dick. Panic began to set in. Then Gigi spoke once more, her voice a husky purr that went right to my balls. "We're starting off my set with a song from the incomparable Josephine Baker titled, simply, 'Paris.'"

She began to sing in French.

The world as I had known it for over twenty-five years tipped and tumbled off its axis, crashing to my feet like a fine china cup tipped from a counter by a mischievous kitten. There was nothing outside of the singer and her song. *His* song. He was a male, despite how feminine he appeared on stage. Gigi Patel LeBay had balls. Balls and a cock. My thoughts slipped into that forbidden place where my yearnings for men were kept locked down tight. My homosexuality was like the dread wolf. Forever chained for the good of all. If anyone found out I was gay, my future would be ruined. No NHL contract, no money to send to my aunt and uncle. No name on the Cup. No keeping my word, my *oath*, to my father.

"I have to piddle," Janine said. All the girls moved off as one down a darkened corridor, returning ten minutes later with tales of being able to peek into the queens' dressing room as they returned from the bathrooms. The whole time they'd been gone, I'd been buried under memories and past pledges. "You want to go?" Janine asked, shaking me from the vows made beside a death bed.

"What? No," I snapped. Her soft blue eyes widened. "Sorry, no, I'm enjoying the show."

"Okay, I just thought you might want to sneak out and go to my place." Her pert ass slide back and forth against my rigid cock. I nearly swallowed my tongue. I jerked my dick from her backside, blabbering something in Danish that she couldn't begin to understand. "You're so shy," she said with a smile as I put some distance between my prick and her ass.

"You smell good," I blabbed in English. Her gaze lit up at the compliment. Maya said something to her then, thank the gods, and her attention moved from me. I fumbled for my drink; my sight locked on the lights above the stage. The lemon-lime soda did little to wash away my erection, but it did cool my throat. Perhaps I should leave now. With Janine. Let the guys think we were going to go fuck, then drop her off with a peck on the cheek. I always had an excuse for cutting out early. Morning skate usually worked, or that I was exhausted from a game. So far she'd bought it, which was a relief. I really did like Janine. She was the perfect hockey player date.

My gaze flitted from the stage lights to the exposed brick walls to the bar to the door of the men's room just visible down a long hallway. I studied the club, looking at the patrons and the posters on the walls. Anywhere and anything other than Gigi. Then, the song about Paris ended to outrageous applause. My friends all clapped. Aside from Ben, who was obviously uncomfortable. He really was a hateful person. Why did we even associate with him off the ice?

"Thank you," Gigi purred. The soda lying in my belly, on top of the far-too-rare beef from the awards banquet, began to froth and bubble. That voice was enchanting. Soft like a woman's, but with a manly undertone. I burped softly as my whole being zeroed in on Gigi at the microphone. "You're all too kind. I'm so happy to be back in Wilmington. As you know, I was on the road with my sisters doing an east coast tour. Imagine, if you will, six bitches with a hundred suitcases each crammed into a 1990 Chevy van for four weeks. Anytime we stopped for gas, every alley cat within a hundred-mile radius appeared. We fondly nicknamed our ride the Fish Mobile!"

The crowed howled in amusement. I had no clue what she—damn it—*he* was talking about. What did fish have to do with people in an old van?

"She's funny," Janine shouted over her shoulder. I nodded because not to nod would make me look stupid. My date moved back a bit, just enough to wiggle tight to me. I slid an arm around her middle, held her close to my hip, but my eyes were now back on Gigi. Her mannerisms were so flowy. She had no masculine traits at all. Yet, she was a he under all that makeup. It was intriguing beyond logic. I wanted to speak with her, hear her say my name in the husky purr, feel her gloved hands on my skin, see my cock slip between those ruby red lips of hers. "I'm having so much fun tonight. I really enjoy dating you."

"Yeah, me too." Gigi had begun a new song. Something old sounding. It made me think of my father. He loved old things. Music, cars, mythology. Which was how I came to be named after the Norse god of war. The screen behind Gigi changed from a soggy Parisian street to a sultry, red velvet background. She wet her lips. A shiver raced down my spine. Then, she leaned into the mic, a fall of soft, lilac hair slipping down to hide her left eye. With a small hand, she pushed it back, and I nearly took a bite out of my glass. Soda ran down my chin. I wiped it away with the back of my hand as one would drool. Hell, it could have *been* drool. All I could think of was brushing a fall of lilac hair back from a heart-shaped face.

Ben began to grumble. We all hushed him so we could

hear Gigi, so he ordered shots that no one but him drank. He'd be sloshed in no time. He tended to drink far too much when he had the opportunity. I gave Ben a look that he ignored, then Gigi caught my eye again. Had she ever truly lost it?

She had a hell of a voice. It was obvious she was not lip-syncing the words, but merely singing along with prerecorded music. Or at least I was pretty sure that was the case. Even if the voice was someone else's, she commanded the stage. I could not look away. And so there I stood, nursing a Sprite, my date slowly forgotten as Gigi went from one old song to another. Far too soon, her set was done. She bowed and threw kisses to the crowd before leaving the stage as the patrons packed into the club gave her a standing ovation. The older queen, Sitka, the one with the red dress and beehive, reappeared.

"Are you gagged?" she asked, and the crowd all stomped their feet. "That's my daughter," she crowed in a voice that sounded ravaged by time and cigarettes. I blinked at the big man on stage. So father and son were both drag queens? What were the odds of that? "The house of Patel always lights up the stage, hunties." The crowd laughed. "Now, we're turning the spotlight over to one of the Northeast's most famous boogers." Laughter filled the club. Ben mumbled something behind me, but I blocked him out as I searched the crowd for Gigi. Would she come out and mingle? Should I go look for her to tell her how amazing her set had been? "Give it up for my dear friend and fellow fossil, Madame Ivy Tote!"

"Dude, *really*?" I heard Dante sniff. I glanced behind me to see Ben splayed out over the bar, his cheek resting in a puddle of booze. "Stupid fuck. Come on, Hems, let's get him home."

The urge to slap the living shit out of Ben was strong. Manhandling a drunk was not on my agenda. I wanted to find Gigi and speak with her. I had no clue what I would say. Something stupid, I was sure.

Gather up Ben and go home. Before someone sees you drooling over a dude in a dress.

Yes. Of course. I needed to go. What had I even been thinking? Dante and I each took an arm, then hoisted our drunken teammate out of his stool and out the door. Ben came around a bit as we were hustling him through the club. Maybe it would have been better if he stayed passed out, because the things he grunted at people we passed made me ashamed to be with him.

"Shut the fuck up," Dante spat when Ben called a lesbian couple something vile. Ben shoved at a dude. The dude shoved back. Thankfully, we were near the front door. I shot a look back at the stage. Gigi was staring at us with dark eyes filled with disgust. We jostled him outside, then shoved him against the wall of the club. I kept a hand on Ben's chest until his ride came.

"Can you take the girls home?" I asked of Dante. "I'll tuck this moron into his bed."

"Sure can." Dante gave me a short hug, then herded the ladies toward an Uber that Janine had hired. She gave me a sad little wave before she was pulled into the sedan. I waved back, then poured Ben into the back of the Toyota.

The ride was short and silent. Ben had drifted off as soon as his ass had hit the seat. When we pulled up, I asked the driver to wait, then wrangled Ben into his condo. He mouthed off a bit when I took his keys, but the bile flowing from him lessened when he faceplanted on his sofa. I tugged off his shoes and loosened his tie before locking the door behind me.

The inside of the Toyota was warm. The driver turned to look back at me when his query about where I wanted to go fell on deaf ears. I wanted to go back to Campo Royale. Desperately.

"14th and Honeywell," I said instead, and fell back into the seat with a sigh of relief. Going home was the smart option. Funny, it didn't feel smart. It just felt empty.

Chapter Two

ELIJAH

THE SHARP FOUR RAPS ON MY TINY DRESSING ROOM DOOR
pulled my attention from the reapplication of my powder.
The lights on stage had melted it off.

"Yes, Mother," I yelled as I dusted my chin. Sitka
slipped in the door, closed it, and then immediately fished
inside her gargantuan wig for a cigarette. I scowled at her
in the lighted mirror propped up on an old desk. "Do *not*
light that thing up in here."

"Such an ungrateful cow you are," she replied with
zero emotion. People thought her cold and unfeeling, but I
knew better. If not for Sitka, I'd have spent a few hungry,
cold years on the streets before my brother came home and
took me in. "Children are such a burden." She stuffed the
wrinkled Marlboro back into her wig, then sat down on
the only chair in the broom closet I had claimed as mine.
With all the racks of gowns and dresses there wasn't room
for anything other than a chair, a desk, and an oscillating
fan. "Hank not coming tonight?"

I shook my head. Sitka leaned back in the ratty, old

chair then crossed one long, thin leg over the other, her pump falling off her heel to dangle from her toes.

"He's working the night shift."

"If I were twenty years younger and had more of an inclination, I'd go break into that office building he guards just so he'd frisk me."

I rolled my eyes. "My brother is straight."

"Your point?" she asked as she fanned her face with her hand.

"He's a security guard. I don't think they frisk people, just secure them and call the cops."

Her lips pulled up into a naughty smile. "Everyone needs a little security."

I shook my head. "You old, horny goat." I wiggled around on my stool. My tuck was killing me, but I had to go mingle in full drag for another hour. "Speaking of security, what was taking place on the floor during my set?"

"A small party of straights. Hockey players from that minor league team of ours."

"We have a hockey team?" I placed my puff back into my case, then began searching for my pink lipstick.

"We do. The Warthogs. They're the feeder team for the Chicago Mules. They have that big brute Tyr Hemmingsen, the war god of Wilmington, they call him. Surely you saw him? He tends to stand out in a crowd. Hulking stud, beard, eyes full of pain and loneliness."

"Oh right, the hulking bearded stud god. I think I might have noticed him." I glanced up at the looking glass. "And you know this how? You hate jocks and sport as much as I do."

"I dated one of them a few years back." My eyes

flared. Sitka smiled mischievously. "Fine. Many years back. Oh, it was all in secret. There is no bigger den of repressed homosexuality than professional sports. He was married. Gasp. I know. This was before I found Jesus." I snorted loudly. Sitka placed a hand over her big, fake breast. "I'm shocked and hurt that you question my religiosity."

"Sorry, Sister Sitka. Do continue. I'm fascinated to hear about your foray into the world of athletic supporters."

She waved a finger at me. "You're being sassy." I smiled sweetly at the looking glass, then resumed looking for my damn pink lipstick. "It was short. The relationship, that is, not his dick."

"I knew we'd come back to cock," I sniggered, then opted to use a lighter pink instead of the one I'd used earlier. I bet Monique had slipped in and stole it. That bitch was always pilfering my makeup.

"The world revolves around it. Anyway, we were an item for about a month. He had tremendous thighs, and a cock that could be seen from space." She sighed dreamily. "Sadly, his wife discovered one of my false eyelashes stuck to his ass. Oops. Needless to say, he never called again. I was inconsolable."

"For a day."

"At least. So that's how I know about hockey. All he did was fuck and talk hockey. Ask me who scored the most points in the Warthog organization in 1997."

"Do I have to?" I carefully applied more color.

"You do."

A sigh leaked out between my freshly painted lips. "Who scored the most points in the Warthog organization in 1997?"

"Clyde. That was his name. Clyde Pinkens. He was a beast. Did I mention his cock?"

"Several times."

"Hmm, well, that's the only thing about him that I recall. That and the stats. Anyway, they were hockey players. I heard Cord behind the bar saying something about one being the team war god?"

Cord, aka Corduroy, was our resident sports guy. The only one of us here who gave two shits about balls that weren't found in trousers. He was a big fan of all the sports, which was why he could talk with the straight men who wandered in on occasion.

What a damn pity. Tall, dark, and sexy had caught my eye the moment I'd seen him at the bar. At first, I'd assumed he was straight given how the woman he stood next to had been staking a claim with every glance and touch. Yet, even as his hand rested on her hip, those smoky eyes of his had lingered on me. Which sent my gaydar into overdrive and also made being tucked slightly uncomfortable. I'd quickly gotten my libido in check, and the twitching down south soon stopped.

"Hockey is so violent. Did you happen to see Monique wearing Pink Petal Number 8 tonight?" I turned my face left, then right, for one final inspection. Fuck, but my balls ached. Untucking sounded marvelous. Shame I had another hour before I could clock out.

"Your makeup is beat, as you well know, so stop working the mirror and get out there and work the crowd. They're all dying to have their Gigi time. They missed you madly."

I turned around on my stool. Sitka stared at me with wide, brown eyes. "Did you miss me, Mother?"

Her lips pursed. "Did you go somewhere?" She tossed it out blithely, but I knew the truth. She was my drag mother. Of course she had missed me. Mother Patel missed all her children when they were gone. "And yes, Monique was in pink. It made her look like a fungi. Which I mentioned, but she chose to ignore."

"I hope her lips puff up like they did the last time she stole my stuff."

"Poor sow couldn't walk properly for a week." I giggled. "We really shouldn't talk about your sister so badly." She smiled that quick, little twitch of a smile before reaching down to slide her pump back on. "My feet are so swollen. I'll have to soak my toes in beans when I get home."

"Do not continue with that joke." She batted fake lashes at me while striking an innocent look. "You were going to say human beans. I know you. I lived with you for two years until Hank left the Corp. That innocent look will not work on me."

"Such a brat." She wedged her toes back into her pump, then stood. "Finish touching up. You have a shiny nose. Then meet me at the bar for a cranberry and vodka."

"Yes, Mother."

I spun back to my little mirror to check my nose. It wasn't the least bit shiny, but it did need a little less contouring. The light in here was dreadful, but ever since that incident with Mona McKenzie and her bag pipes, I refused to use the communal room. A girl had to have some privacy away from insane Scots who insisted on piping in your ear. Besides, I had earned this damn broom closet. I'd busted my ass here at the Royale for the past four years. I'd started out as a bus boy as I learned my craft from Sitka. Those had been hard times. I'd left home at sixteen, and Hank was in the Marine Corp, stationed over in Okinawa at Camp Butler. If not for Sitka taking me in off the streets…well, I would probably be selling blowjobs behind the Quik-Pick Mart instead of dressing up in beautiful clothes, wearing makeup, and singing old romance songs.

Slowly, I'd worked my way to the stage and now I was the headliner, despite what Monique thought. I was one grand tour from making it big. I could *feel* my future was about to change and I was ready for whatever destiny brought my way!

IT WAS close to noon the next day when I rolled around in my bed, eyes squinty, as my brother's damn phone rang out in the living room.

"Please, by all that is holy, change your ringtone," I groaned as I stumbled out of bed in my flannel bottoms to find his phone. I hated the old-fashioned, *bring-bring-bring* tone he used. He kept it just to annoy the piss out of me, I was sure. I knew he'd not hear it. He slept with his TV on: *Finding Dory* on a steady loop. It was the only way his brain would power down, he claimed. I thought that he just adored the film, but, being a big, bad ex-Marine, he couldn't cop being in love with a kid's film.

Bumbling through the small ranch home he'd bought with a loan from the VA, I followed the annoying ringing until I located his work jacket. "Masterson Security" was proudly stitched across the back of the navy-blue coat. His work pants and shirt were the same boring color. Honestly, if I had to wear that mundane outfit day in and day out, I would slit my throat with a nail file.

I dug his cell out of his coat pocket, frowned at the four-percent charge left on it, and then groaned when I saw who was calling. Steeling myself, I answered the call from my mother.

"Henry, I was about to hang up and call the police. I've been calling you for the past four hours," Mom clucked.

"Mom, it's Eli," I slipped into her tirade.

"Oh."

Yeah, good morning to you, too, Mother. "Hank worked the night shift last night. He's on that new swing shift they set up."

"Oh, yes, of course." I slid over the back of our well-used sofa and tugged the throw Hank's girlfriend Becky had crocheted for him. The stitches were all wonky and the bright green color clashed with everything in the world, but Becky had made it, so I pulled it around my bare shoulders. It worked well to ward off the incoming chill.

"So yeah, he's asleep." I tucked my naked toes under my ass and stared at the dusty entertainment center.

"He works incredibly hard."

"Yeah, he does. I do, too. I was working last night. I just got back from a tour of the eastern states. It was a big success. Lots of the fans are following me on social media now."

You could too, Mom.

"When will Henry wake up do you think?"

Ouch. That hurt. Fuck me for allowing it to hurt. Damn it. "Probably not until three or so."

"Leave him a note to call home."

"Yep. Will do." I waited for her to say something. Anything. But no. The line went dead. Burrowing under the lopsided, green blanket I stared at my hands resting in my lap, Hank's nearly dead cell cradled in my palms. Tears threatened, but I forbid them to break free. I'd shed enough tears over my parents. I swiped at my cheeks. Damn it. I was such a weakling.

"Hey, are you jerking off in there?" Hank asked, whipping the cover off of my head. My sky-blue hair crackled with static.

"Mom called. She wants to talk to you." I held his phone over my head. "Plug it in, please."

He took the phone, then slung a thick leg over the back of the sofa, plopping down beside me with a grunt. His arm looped around my neck. I let my head fall to his wide shoulder. Hank was the son every parent wants. Outgoing, athletic, straight. He'd been a fullback on our football team back in Bradford, Pennsylvania. Or was that a running back? Well, it was some kind of back. He'd been good but had opted to join the Marines after graduation. Served his country, left the Corp with a glowing record, and came to Wilmington to find me. I wasn't exactly hiding. He knew where I was and who I was living with as we'd stayed in contact during his time overseas. He fully accepted me and my sexuality, as well as my drive to be a drag performer. Hell, Hank was the one who fitted out my sewing room once we had moved in here. He was my backbone and my strength. No gay kid could ask for a better, more loving brother. Hank made up for the cold indifference from my parents.

"Hey, fuck them, right?" He gave me a brotherly squeeze. I nodded. He tightened the hug.

"Yeah, fuck them."

"You want something to eat? I could eat." He rustled my knotted hair then got to his feet. I gave him a short bob of my head. "Cool. Go find a shirt and join me in the kitchen. I feel like an omelet."

"Funny, you don't look like an omelet." He rolled his eyes. "Thank you. I'll be here all week. Make sure to tip your servers."

"Asshole." He walked off chuckling. I waited until he was in the kitchen rattling pans before I scrubbed at my face with my hands so hard it made my nose ache. I knew Hank was right. Fuck them. If they couldn't accept me, then fuck them. I had other family. That was one of the blessings of being a gay person. You made your own family. I had Hank, Becky, Sitka, and all the other bitches at the club, many who were also daughters of Patel. Even Monique. Why did I care if my mother and father refused to come see my shows? It was their loss. I was fucking amazing.

"I'm fucking amazing!" I shouted out loud.

"You rock. Now come butter the toast, superstar!" Hank called from the kitchen.

Superstar. Yeah, well, not quite, but soon. I hoped. God, how I hoped.

I ARRIVED at the Campo by two in the afternoon after stopping for an iced coffee. The doors didn't open until six for early cocktails, and because Sitka, who owned the club, refused to leave his bed before noon. Thankfully, he had managers who handled the day-to-day for him, as he had no wish to fuck with receipts and such. He simply wanted to run the shows and be the master of ceremonies.

Padding in the back way as always, I stopped by the communal dressing room, but it was empty. The lighted tables were dark. The laughter and/or catfighting that took place in this room nightly was thankfully silent. For now. Give it a few hours. I stopped at my broom closet to change from jeans and a purple hoodie into leggings, a sweater, and heels. With my drink in hand, I made my way through the darkened halls that led to the main stage. There waited the other girls who were taking part in the Campo Royale Halloween Extravaganza. Monique, my drag sister and pilferer of pink lip gloss, gave me a searing look.

"Don't even start," I snapped at her as I climbed onto the stage.

"We were supposed to be here at one," she started. Did I not ask her to not do that? "Just because you're mother's little tartlet, that doesn't mean you can sashay your skinny ass in here whenever you wish."

I took a loud slurp of my iced coffee. "Fuck off, bitch." She gasped as if slapped.

"Okay, can we skip the catfight? I just got my nails done, and I'll be damned if I snap one off breaking up you two bitches," Clarise said, then took me by the elbow and steered me around a glowering Monique. "Honestly, child, you need to pick which hill to die on. Why do you even engage? You know that bitch is sick with envy."

"I know. She just tugs my gaff."

Clarice drew back and looked down at my package. "You could use your gaff, henny."

That made me chuckle. I loved Clarice Patel Coco, aka

Leroy Marx, so much. He was our stage manager when Sitka wasn't here. The leggy, Black queen was in her late thirties, funny as shit, and about as sweet a soul as was humanly possible.

I threw my hands over my junk then giggled like a true coquette. Trust me, there were no secrets here. These bitches knew everything about me just as I did them. We worked together six nights a week, we toured together, hell, we even shaved our balls then tucked them together.

There were four of us here this afternoon. We were the headliners who had been invited to take part in the holiday show. Tickets usually sold well, but Sitka always kept a few spares for the rich and famous. Not that Wilmington had rich and famous, exactly. Although, the mayor was known to drop by on occasion but always watched the show from backstage, then went off to have drinks with Monique. His wife was not aware of the shows or the cocktails with the six-foot-three-inch drag queen. My lips remained sealed. There was a line that we Patel sisters did not cross, even if we disliked each other. Sisters before misters.

"Can we queue up Gigi's number, please?" Monique huffed from her side of the stage. "I have things to do before the show tonight, and we've been delayed already."

I glanced at Clarice, who rolled her dark eyes, then walked over to fiddle with the sound system. I placed my iced coffee on the edge of the stage, ran my fingers through my hair, and stalked to center stage. The other three would be backup dancers for my numbers, then I would return the favor. Which meant that we all had to memorize the words and dance routines for twenty numbers. Our bits would be broken up with comedy queens and kings. We spent an hour rehearsing their songs and the chorography that went with them, then we moved to my set.

The empty club came alive with the opening notes of "Punky Punkin," a classic Halloween song voiced by the amazing Rosemary Clooney. Monique groaned at the music. She loathed my 40s and 50s aesthetic, but the fans certainly ate it up, so screw the jealous cow bag. She also couldn't carry a tune, so the fact that she had to sing instead of lip-sync as she preferred twisted her nuts tightly. Could I have lip-synced? Sure. But my supporters loved my voice, so she could just bray along in the background as she always did.

We moved right into "Witchcraft" afterward. Then followed that by a bouncy rendition of "The Wobblin Goblin," also made famous by Rosemary Clooney, then slid into "The Walls Keep Talking" before we worked on "Haunted Heart," a slow, sad song by Frances Langford. Given the era of my chosen music, the backup girls had little to do aside from sing and sway. It wasn't as strenuous dancing as it was for the others who had chosen tunes from Rihanna, Michael Jackson, Beyoncé, Missy Elliott, and The Black Keys. I was soaked with sweat, and my feet ached from being in heels even if they were old, worn heels.

Amazingly, things went smoothly with only a few missteps and forgotten lyrics until the very end: when Monique "accidentally" kicked my iced coffee off the stage.

"If your feet weren't the size of water skis, maybe that wouldn't happen," I spat then huffed away to find a mop. When I returned, the stage was empty aside from the cleaning crew and Clarice, who was trying to clean up the mess with soggy bar napkins. "Here, let me get this." I pulled the mop bucket along behind me, my heels hitting the old, wooden dance floor like hammer strikes. "Where did the others go?"

Clarice stood then dropped the soggy napkins into a trash can by the stage. "Monique and said it was time enough spent on this. She said she had enough of your stupid-ass, old, bougee shit."

"She wouldn't know class if it shimmied up under her too-tight skirt and took up residence in her anal passage," I grunted while slapping a mop across the floor. "What is her problem, cracking her neck at me all the time?"

"You know what it is. She hates the fact that a twinkly, little newcomer has nudged her out of the limelight of the tours and Mother Sitka's brassy heart. You'll want to watch your back. The things she was saying about you to the other girls when you were gone…" I looked up from the wet mopping. Clarice bit down on the inside of her cheek. She rarely spoke ill of anyone, so this warning was to be taken seriously. "I'm not repeating what was said because it was untruths, but just keep her in front of you, or she will kick your sweet ass off the stage just like she did your iced coffee."

Great. So not only was my "sister" jealous of my taking her place on tour and here in the club, she also had been badmouthing me behind my back. I wasn't about to back down. Not to a rude sow like Monique Marshall. She could bring it. I wasn't scared. I might be tiny, but I was mighty.

Chapter Three

TYR

Eight days had passed since *that* night.

That night that had spun me in circles.

That night that I'd first laid eyes on Gigi Patel LeBay.

Gigi had been in my dreams nightly. Which meant that I woke up with a raging hard-on every morning. If I'd been home, I could have taken care of it with my hand and a lot of spit. But we'd not been home. We'd been in Connecticut for back-to-back games with the Hartford Howlers then made a stop in Salem for a game. Alone time simply didn't happen when you roomed with your line mate. I loved Dante, I really did, but ten fucking minutes to myself would have been greatly appreciated. My buddy talked. A lot. All the time. Even when I was in the hotel bathroom, his mouth was going about something. Usually nonsense, but still, his voice floating into the bathroom while I stood in the shower with my dick in my hand killed any kind of amorous thoughts. There was no escaping him or the other Warthogs. We were together twenty-four and seven. Sharing rooms, sharing charter buses, sharing meals.

I'd never been happier to get home in my life. My feet had barely crossed the threshold of my little second-floor apartment when my phone rang in my back pocket. I dropped my bags to the floor as my brain skipped ahead to the thought of a good tug. Then I saw that it was my Aunt Alma calling. All stirrings below the belt stalled immediately.

I drew in a breath and braced myself before answering the call. I loved my aunt, I did, and I would do whatever she wanted whenever she wanted it. She and my uncle Jens had taken me in when my mother had committed suicide a year after my father had passed. I'd failed my father's dying requests in that manner, as well. Sometimes, when I was tired and confused as I was now, I wished our lives were different. I wished I hadn't been born who and what I was. But that was not how the Norns had laid out my fate at birth.

"Hello," I said with as much cheer as I could muster. I really was exhausted and sore. The games in Hartford had been incredibly physical. I'd taken a beating along the boards from their defense. But paybacks would come. They'd be on my ice in two weeks. I'd have my head sorted and my dick under control by then.

"Hello, Tyr," she said in Danish. I braced myself for a five-minute call filled with little substance or emotion. Aunt Alma and Uncle Jens were not demonstrative people. "Tell me about hockey and America. Any news on the girlfriend front?"

"No, no news." That was my standard reply. Then I neatly led her away from the girlfriend talk into hockey.

We chatted for another few minutes, then she had to go vacuum, so the call ended. It was a blessing.

How I wished I'd somehow made my mother get treatment. She had gone untreated for her bipolar depression for so long her mind had seemed to be hardwired into the horrifying pattern of highs and lows. Losing my father had pushed her into a funk that she never climbed out of. I'd found her dead in her bed when I was fourteen, sleeping pill bottle by her side. My childless aunt and uncle took me in. I'd not gone hungry or been cold. They'd clothed me, taken me to hockey games and tournaments, lugged me to college, and done what was necessary. But they were not my parents. They'd never wanted kids, and it was obvious. Not that they were cruel, they weren't, they simply did not want me in their house but they were bound by blood.

I sat there, staring out the window, my phone in my palm. A drowning sort of darkness lurked just outside the window. It always appeared after a talk with my aunt. The creature crept around on the periphery of my life, and it terrified me. Was it perhaps mental illness looking for a chink in the war god's armor? Maybe it was just the sadness that hearing my aunt stirred within me. She and my mother did speak in the same manner.

I thought of calling Janine, but I knew that she was working a late shift at the hospital. I did not want to pull Nurse Briggs from a patient with my blues. I knew firsthand how important nurses were to their patients. Also, it wasn't Janine that I wanted to see. She hadn't entered my thoughts for a week. How could she when Gigi Patel LeBay had taken all the room inside my skull? The old notebooks on the bookshelf called to me.

Perhaps I could sit and write. It had been so long, but perhaps if I started small. A short fable or a quick tale about a magical fox. Thinking of sitting down with a pencil and paper warmed me. How I had loved to create stories when I was younger. Fairy tales were my favorites. Stories filled with heroes, villains, magic, a fantasy setting and, of course, a moral at the end. Somehow, after the move to my aunt and uncle's, I managed to hold onto the old notebooks crammed with fables I had created.

They'd been hidden in my closet, for my father forbade me to waste my time writing about fairy tales when there was hockey practice. Maybe I could sit down now and tell a tale of a magical fish and a handsome prince who catches it only to find out it's a prince from another land who had been hexed by a witch. Yes, maybe it would ease the ache of being alone for a bit. I warred with myself for a whole of ten seconds then rushed out of my lonely apartment and grabbed the next bus across town.

The lights of Campo Royale Club were bright and alluring. My gaze lingered on the big neon lips. My heart began a strange, tapping dance inside my chest. I should not have come here. I knew that now. Any other Warthog would have called his girl to set up a date for later tonight for sex, if they hadn't grabbed some on the road. There were always plenty of offers. I tugged on my hat, pulling the blue beret that matched my navy suit. I'd not even changed when I got home, I just noticed. Not that I had to wear a suit to the games or when we were travelling, but it seemed like a good practice to get into. Also, they looked good on me.

There I stood on a chilly corner, pulse thundering, staring at the flashy red lips as a war for my soul waged inside me. Funny how the moniker I had been given at birth was not helping me win this battle. One shuffling step at a time I felt the pull of the club and the diminutive performer inside. I *hoped* she was inside. When I was in front of the doorman, I kept my eyes down, my beret riding on my eyebrows, and handed over the cover charge.

"Is Gigi performing tonight?" I asked over the shouts and thumps that were sneaking out into the autumn air. I glanced up in time to see the doorman nod before he motioned me along. Desire rushed through me as I snuck inside. The club was alive, it seemed. The air thick with laughter and perfume. I drew it in, and it tingled as it moved into my lungs. My sight flew to the stage, but I knew it wasn't Gigi simply by the music. The performer on stage wasn't singing as Gigi did, she was simply moving her lips to a 90s song from Belinda Carlisle. She was good, but she wasn't Gigi. My dick was half-hard, and my breathing skittish, when I found a small table for two that had recently been vacated. Guess Thursday nights were slow. A server arrived, clad, like the bartenders, in rainbow suspenders and a black crop top. She was so tall she had to bend over in half to hear my order. Her hair was pulled back into a ponytail. She smelled good and gave me a slow appraisal as I asked for a Sprite with extra ice.

Once she was gone, I slouched down in my seat, shoulders up and beret nearly in my eyes. I sat through the 90s homage then clapped politely for the queen on stage, Monique, as she exited the stage. The lights dimmed. The screen was now showing what looked like vintage wallpaper pale pink with tiny, dark-pink roses. My grandmother had a bathroom with similar paper in her old house. I took a sip of my soda, unsure of…well, unsure of everything. Until the music started. Then, I was sure that this seat was where I needed to be. Gigi stepped onto the stage in a pink dress with white dots. Her hair was the same color as the wallpaper behind her, a cotton-candy-pink that looked soft as down. It was swirled up to bare her long, thin neck. My mouth went dry. I gulped some of soda as she took the microphone between her tiny hands as gently as if it were a fledgling fallen from a nest.

"Good evening," she breathlessly said into the mic. My body went haywire. My heart sped up, my palms went dry, my cock swelled. "Tonight, I'm going to try out a few new songs for you." She stepped closer to the mic, her lean calves tapering down to a finely-boned ankle and foot. Her shoes were light-pink and her little toes peeked out of them. Even her toenails were pink. I took another drink, then another, as she lowered the microphone. Then her eyes met mine. Her lashes were long and thick, her eyes painted to subtle perfection with bold lines and deep, rose shadows. "Hello, handsome, enjoying the view?" she asked then lifted her skirt to show off her stockings. And a garter belt. Dear gods. I'd never seen a more beautiful thigh in all my life.

The crowd tittered at me sitting there like a goon. "It's a most stunning sight," I forced out. Gigi smiled, but it didn't quite reach her deep, brown eyes.

"'Stunning,' he says. Hmm, that makes me think of a song. Do you want a song?" she asked me, or it seemed as if she were speaking to me. I nodded like a dullard. Her gaze lingered for just a moment on me before she began singing. I was lost. Utterly, fully bewildered and enchanted. I have to speak to her, just once, to tell her…I had no clue, but I needed to speak to her. "Let's kick off my set with a little Billie Holiday's 'Crazy He Calls Me.'"

I nodded as if I knew who Billie Holiday was. She wet her dark-pink lips then began to sing. The hour rushed by, one song after another, each captivating me. Silken strands of words and music that ensnared me, neatly. I was willingly her captive. I never once looked at anything else but Gigi. Then, as if she had been one of those night mirages that had drifted through my dreams, she was gone. A curtsy and then nothing. The lights on the stage went out, the screen went dark, and the patrons all turned back to their dates.

I pushed to my feet and made my way to the long hallway that led to the bathrooms and dressing area. I got as far as the men's room before meeting resistance. A man the size of an upright freezer was seated on a stool just the other side of the bathrooms. He looked me up and down with steely eyes.

"Don't even think about it," he stated emotionlessly.

"I only wanted to speak to Gigi," I replied. Boredom oozed off him in waves. He slowly got to his feet. He had me by a few inches and perhaps thirty pounds. I glanced around his formidable girth at the row of doors just beyond reach.

"You and half the poor slobs out there. Go back to your seat. Gigi will be out as soon as she changes into something more comfortable." He jerked his bald head at the main seating area. I probably could have taken him. He was huge, yes, but soft and old. I'd thrown down with enforcers close to his size. Everyone who knew how to throw a punch wanted to take on the war god of Wilmington. "I know what you're thinking, big guy." My sight flew back to his broad, flat face. "You try it, and you'll be tossed out on the street and banned from ever coming back into the club. Choice is yours."

"I'll go back to my table."

"Smart man." He jerked his chin at the bar area. I shuffled back to my table like a whipped dog. The server was clearing my glass when I returned.

"Can you bring me another Sprite and whatever it is that Gigi drinks?"

I got a long, pathetic look that I didn't understand. "Sure thing," she sighed then made her way to the bar. I sat down, pulled at my suit to work out the wrinkles, and waited for another forty minutes for Gigi to appear. I shot to my feet as soon as she entered the club in a long, punch-colored lounging robe that swept the floor. Her sight darted around the club then landed on me. I motioned to the vodka and cranberry that the server had brought. The ice was mostly melted. It had taken her much longer to change than I'd assumed it would. My hand shook a bit, I noticed, so I hurried and shoved it into my front pocket.

She moved through the smallish crowd, stopping to talk and laugh with her followers. I waited, standing, until she was standing at my table. Her chin was tilted upward and her eyes were big, dark-chocolate wells outlined with black liner. I'd never seen such long, thick lashes on a person before. The sweep of those lashes when she blinked mesmerized me. As did the way her mouth was formed, the gentle roundness of her chin, and the way she held her head. She was regal. I fumbled around mentally, searching for something to say. When nothing popped into my head, I reached for her hand, bent over it, and kissed her perfumed knuckles. Her skin was soft as satin. When I straightened, her eyes were wide.

"How flattering," she said as I held her tiny hand in mine. "Do you think I'm some sort of nobility?"

"I think you're more beautiful than Princess Marie."

"I don't know who that is," she confessed while her fingers lingered in mine.

"She's married to Prince Joachim."

"Don't know him, either." Her gaze dipped to the cocktail on the table. "Is that for me?"

"Yes, but it's watery. Let me get you another." I released her hand to wave at my server. Then I hurried to pull a chair out for her. "Please, sit. I'll tell you all about the royal family of Denmark. I met Princess Marie once at a charity event."

Gigi gave me a bored smile but did deposit her tiny backside into the chair. I gently pushed her in while cursing myself for my stupidity. As if this beautiful queen wanted to hear about the Danish royal family. I was a moron.

I dropped down into my seat after the drinks were delivered. Gigi lifted hers to her pink lips and took a sip. I watched her throat work. She did have a noticeable Adam's apple which I longed to press my lips against.

"So, tell me about how I out-regal this princess you once met." Her dark eyes sparkled.

And so I began talking. About the queen and her sister, their children and grandchildren, and the eight-hundred-year history of the Dannebrog, what we called our flag.

"…that's how during a battle in 1219 in Estonia our flag was delivered from us."

She studied me over her nearly empty glass. "So you're

telling me that a red flag with a white cross just fell from the sky, and that changed the luck of the Danish army?"

"So the story goes." I wished I had something witty to say. All my wit had flown the coop, not that I had a lot to begin with.

"Wow. Our flag was made by Betsy Ross."

"Actually, that's not true," I blurted out then bit down on my tongue when her eyes flared. "I'm a bit of a history buff. That story didn't appear until the 1870s. That's at least a hundred years after the first American flag was created. It was put forth by a grandson of Betsy Ross. They say that, while Ross *did* make flags in that time period, the story about her actually creating the flag is a myth."

Gigi lowered her glass. "So you're a history nerd." I nodded slowly, my face warm from embarrassment. "That's...actually kind of adorable."

My ears were now hot. "Thank you." I stared openly at her, trying to see the man under all the makeup. He had to be stunning. I wondered what his name was. Did I dare ask? "How do I address you?" She smiled softly at me and all reason flew out the window.

"Your majesty will work," she replied with a wink. I gaped, then the joke finally hit the mark. A smile tugged at my lips. Her eyes dropped to my mouth for a second. "When I'm in drag, you call me Gigi. When I'm not in drag, you call me by my given name."

"Will you tell me your given name?"

"Will you tell me yours?"

"Tyr Hemmingsen."

"What a buff name." I didn't know how to reply. "My name is Eli."

"Short for Elijah?" Her head bobbed. "But you are now Gigi."

"That's right. You are incredibly cute for a bloodcurdling war machine."

I smiled a bit. "I'm only bloodcurdling on the ice."

"Mm, I can see that you're a bit of a teddy bear with those soft blushes and stammers."

She had pegged me well. I was so enjoying our talk. I wanted to spend more time with her. The question, "Would you consider having a dinner with me sometime?" rolled out of me before I could even consider the ramifications of such a date.

Her smile flitted away. "Oh honey, that's so cute. I'm flattered, but I don't date fans." With that she rose to her tiny slippers, kissed my cheek, and sailed back to the dressing area. My jaw dropped and my heart sank. The server arrived with a fresh Sprite and a pat on the shoulder.

"Tough break, big guy," she said then made her way back to the bar.

I had no idea how to proceed from here or even if I should. Wise Tyr would tell me to run, not walk, out of this club and never come back. As the warmth from her kiss lingered on my cheek, I strongly suspected that the wise Tyr, the one who was known for justice, was about to be shoved aside by the side of Tyr that had the blood of giants bubbling in its veins.

Chapter Four

ELIJAH

Sitka snuck up on me from behind.

"What are we spying on?" she asked, her voice startling me into a small yelp of fright. I spun around, leaving the sight of the poor, besotted Tyr Hemmingsen staring into his drink to glower up at my mother.

"Nothing." I tugged on the sash around my waist then sailed to my little broom closet, nose in the air. Sitka followed me then pushed into my space, even when I was trying to shut the door on her face. "I need to get out of drag."

"Then do so," she commented as she plopped down into the chair that she always occupied. She was in high drag tonight—her spacy silver lame outfit—due to a fundraising stint in Philly. "I've seen your twig and grapes before."

I tugged at my wig then winced when the spirit gum holding my synthetic wig to my head held tight, pulling at my sideburns. Hissing, I then slowed down and reached for the Vaseline jar.

"You seem out of sorts tonight. Care to talk?" Sitka asked from behind. I shook my head while working Vaseline into the lace wig edging glued to my skin. "Did that big oak tree with legs piss you off?"

I glared at her in my mirror. "How long were you spying?"

"Long enough to see the lovestruck looks on both of your faces." She leaned to the side to get her whole face into the mirror's reflection. I rolled my eyes as I worked at the glue. "Oh yes, dumpling, I saw you drooling all over your robe—which is to die for by the way. Make sure to cover that pretty up."

"Thank you. I got it in Boston. There was no drooling." I reached for my old dollar store granny robe. It was covered with powder, lipstick, concealer, foundation, and so much hairspray the bitch stood in the corner all by itself. It was ugly as sin—gingham was not my pattern— but it was a necessity.

She made a sound that I knew too well. A short snort that told the world she had discovered bullshit. But she hadn't found any to do with me. Yes, I'd been drawn to him. Obviously, that was the case, or I would *not* have had a drink with the man. Usually, I just flittered around from table to table making small talk. I rarely sat with a man because that led to—

"What are mother's rules about fans?" I winced as I eased my wig off. Not because the glue was still sticking, but because I knew she was going to ask. Giving myself a moment, I placed my wig onto a foam head then eased out of my feathered Hollywood robe and into my old granny robe.

"Don't date the fans," I replied with a weary sigh. I

wiped my hands off on a paper towel, removed the pantyhose from my head, and scrubbed at my scalp with my fingernails. One popped off. "Ugh, dirty whore," I huffed, then bent down to pick up the long pink nail from the floor.

"What else?" She prodded the back of my stool with her chunky silver space boot.

"Don't fuck the fans."

"And why do we not engage in dicking and or being dicked by the fans?"

I really wanted to lob a fucking compact at her. "Because we travel too much."

"And?"

"Do we really have to rehash all your old dating rules?" I grabbed my jar of cold cream and slathered some over my cheeks.

"Yes, pudding we do. I saw the 'fuck me in the ass until I forget my name' looks you were giving him."

Ugh. "I was *not* looking at him that way. Sure, he's big, strong, sexy, bearded, and oozes testosterone…" My mind wandered a bit.

"*Elijah.*"

I smeared a glob of cold cream to my forehead. "We don't date fans because we're never sure if they're hot for our stage persona or the real us and we dislike being sexually exploited and or used by a star seeker."

"Very good." She smiled at me. I flipped her off with a cold cream covered middle finger. "Now, don't be a turnip. Those rules are there to protect my children from heartbreak. That man could be into Gigi as a woman and totally not into the man under the wig."

"I know. I know. It's just…" I paused in creaming my

chin. "It's lonely. I'm lonely. I want someone in my life. I'm tired of being alone."

She leaned up to wrap her arms around me. I let my eyes close for a moment. How many times after I'd moved out of my home at sixteen had these strong arms held me while I cried? Thousands, it seemed like.

"It's a hard life being a public figure. You're just at the start of a career that is going to see you reach heights most of us here only dream of. Don't let a pretty face and a big cock keep you from reaching for that brass ring."

I sniffled. "Brass hell! I want platinum, girl."

A short, gruff laugh escaped her. "That's my Gigi. Now get cleaned up and go home." She stood, pecked the top of my head, and then exited my cramped closet. Once the door was closed behind her spacy ass, I sat there staring at myself. Hair standing up, makeup smeared over my face. It always felt so odd to me when I was at this in-between stage of shifting from Gigi to Eli, or vice versa when I was covering Eli to create Gigi. Who was I really? The answer was that I was both. Gigi was a part of Eli. And while I adored her, I didn't want men to want to be with *her* instead of *me*. Which was why Sitka's rules about going out with fans made so much sense. She was always trying to protect us, as a good mother should. Still, I'd been charmed by the huge man in the stupid beret. Tyr had seemed so innocent, yet he couldn't be as he pounded people. And not the fun kind of pounding either, the bloody violent pounding. Yet there had been a tenderness in those light brown eyes as he gazed at me. But he was besotted with Gigi. He didn't know me at all, so it was obviously a case of a straight guy hot for the made-up fantasy of what he thought women should be.

"And who needs that?" I asked myself, then worked on ridding my face of Gigi.

When Eli was staring back at me, I smiled at him. "Hey, welcome back." I booped my nose in the mirror then started removing the padding under my slinky robe. When it was my skinny body bared to the world, I pulled on a pair of jeans and a thick sweater, and stepped into a pair of knockoff Alexander McQueen boots. One day I'd be able to afford the real thing. With my sweater to ward off the chill and my tiny bag on my shoulder, I exited the club via the rear, stopping to yell goodbye to the other girls before stepping out into the frosty night. I checked on the ride that I'd called for, then scampered around front where I ran into the war god waiting for a bus.

He looked my way once, then twice, and then a third time. I waited for the look of bitter disappointment to appear. It never did. Instead, I was given a smile that started small then grew into a grin that melted the thin ice wall that I'd just rebuilt.

"Eli," he said, then took a step closer.

"How did you know it was me?"

"Your eyes, your throat, your lips." My ride pulled up. I shoved my phone into my pink handbag. "I'm sorry. Am I being weird?"

"No. Well, just a little." I opened the back door of the Subaru. "It's a cute weird."

He rubbed at his chin. "I'm catching a bus home. I'm really not stalking you or waiting for you like some sort of…"

"Weird stalker?"

"Yeah."

I suspected he was blushing. That turned me on big

time. He looked cold. Edible. Adorable. Sexy. Fuck. Sitka would boot me in the ass for what I was about to do but sometimes the dick wanted what the dick wanted. And mine was plumping up nicely.

"Want to share a ride?" I asked as the door hung open. His eyebrows climbed up his forehead to hide under his beret. God, that was a stupid hat, but somehow, he made it work. He glanced up and down the street and then nodded. "Then get in. I'm freezing my titties off."

I dove in and Tyr followed, folding himself into origami. He was twice as big in this small space and my dick was now fully into this whatever it was we had going. If Mother only knew what was taking place inside my head, she would literally flip her wig.

"Thanks for sharing the ride," he said in that softly accented voice of his.

I peeked at him sideways. His gaze met and held mine. Lust was billowing off us in waves. One could barely breath due to the pheromones.

"We still going to the original address?" my driver asked, breaking the spell we'd both been caught in.

That was the million-dollar question wasn't it? Did I invite the big, burly, bearded Viking into my home for a drink and some mind-blowing sex? Okay yes, I didn't know for sure the sex would be mind-blowing but given the size of the man's hands he'd be hung like...

"What's a Viking horse?" I asked out of the blue.

"Sleipnir," he instantly answered. "He's an eight-legged horse ridden by Odin."

"Oh, right! The old guy with the eye patch. I remember seeing him in the movie. How I managed to take my eyes off of Hiddleston and Hemsworth long enough to see anyone else is beyond me."

He ducked his head, a smile on his lips. Good Lord, this man was too cute. His personality did not go with his hulking size. I'd always been a trumpet for big grizzly men with the heart of a Care Bear. He was a pure Golden Retriever boy if ever I saw one. I was reaching for his massive hand when the driver cleared his throat. Shit. Yes. He was waiting for directions.

"You can drop me off at my place. 17 Palmetto Drive," Tyr replied. My heart sank and my dick began to droop. Tyr glanced at me moping. "Unless you wish to be dropped off first. I assumed you'd not like me knowing where you live, in case I am a weird stalker."

I waved his worry off. "Honey, if I really thought you were a danger to me, I would not be in this shitty car."

"Hey," the driver barked.

"Sorry, it's a lovely car. I adore it!"

The driver gave me a sour look then pulled from the curb. I sat next to a sexy smelling behemoth for several blocks in utter silence. Sitka's words were slapping me around the entire ride to Tyr's quaint little home.

"I live on the second floor," he said, then pointed at the charming brick two-story townhouse wedged between other charming townhouses. The street was nothing but red brick townhouses, but they were well kept. "My landlord is an old dancer. She plays the kind of music that you sing after dinner every night."

"Fabulous." I sighed as he opened the door then climbed out. Arms folded, eyes on his tasty ass, I plastered on a smile. "She sounds like she has incredible taste in music." He bent down to look into the back.

"Thanks for the ride, Eli. Is it okay if I—" He hit a wall, then, it seemed. His lips flattened. "Thanks for the ride, Eli."

"You're welcome." He stared at me for a moment, then closed the door and jogged up the stairs to a bright white door. Inside he went without a look back. I felt quite slighted.

I heard Sitka inside my head, and she was pissed. Damn it. She was right. Beautiful as he may be, the man had a girlfriend. I'd seen them together at the club. The leggy blonde had made sure that everyone knew that man was hers. I had no clue as to what kind of game he was playing, but I was not into it. Nope. Been there and done that with the straight boys who were looking to dabble on the wigged side until they felt balls in their hand instead of snatch. Then they ran for the hills. Nope. Was not going there again. *Ever*. Not even for big, bearded boys with lips that begged to be tasted.

"Where to now?"

"The original destination," I stated and never once looked back as we drove away. I didn't need to glance in the rearview because I was already over him. It. Over it.

I SLEPT in the next day, rolling out around four in the afternoon after a fitful night of sleep. I had those nights. My brain ran away with me at times. When that happened, I usually got up and designed dresses. The simple act of creation soothed me and occupied my mind, shushing away the outside issues that made me toss and turn. Waking up with a pencil stuck to your cheek was never fun, but the new dress I'd sketched out for the Halloween event was gag worthy.

I had a week to construct it. After a shower, I grabbed a pineapple yogurt and a glass of milk and went into my sewing room. There, I pawed through boxes of old patterns that I'd gathered over the years. Yes, this bitch loved jewelry and flowers from admirers. Nothing won me over like McCall's or Simplicity patterns from the 40s and 50s. They were hard to find, but that was why Hank and I went to auctions and yard sales whenever we could. Thinking of my brother caused him to appear. He stuck his head into the spare room—aka Gigi's Realm of Magnificence—and smiled at me.

"I knew I'd find you in here." I waved at the envelopes scattered around me. "I'd help you but..." He held up the cloth totes filled with groceries.

"Go take care of the food. You don't know the difference between a scoop neck and a Peter Pan collar." I gave him a wink then sat back on my heels.

"True, but I know how to change a tire."

"That's why they invented AAA," I parried as I spooned some yogurt into my mouth.

Hank snickered then padded closer. "I like the blue one."

"I do, too." I hummed around my spoon as I studied the evening dress with cummerbund and detachable overskirt. "Blue's not the right color for Halloween, though." My sight flittered to the bolts of material standing upright in several large plastic totes. "Perhaps purple and black," I mumbled around my spoon. "Maybe the deep purple crêpe georgette with black velvet cummerbund and evening gloves."

"Yeah, sounds good." I threw my brother a look. "You'll look like a skinny bruise."

"Do go away." I waved my spoon at him. He ambled off, chuckling, as I set up to cut material later in the evening. If I could get the pattern pinned and cut tonight, I'd be able to sew tomorrow afternoon. Hank appeared as I was marking the darts.

I glanced up from my table. "Dinner's ready."

"Really?" I checked the kitty kat clock on the wall. Two hours had zipped by. "Okay. I'll be right out."

Thirty minutes later, I made my way to the kitchen to find a pot of spaghetti sauce on the stove and a colander full of angel hair pasta in the sink. After I'd warmed my plate and found a bottle of water in the fridge, I made my way to the living room. Hank was enjoying his night off, feet on the coffee table, beer in hand. I sat down beside him, my gaze moving from the toe sticking out of his sock to the TV then back to his sock.

"Doesn't that bother you?" I asked, then twirled some pasta around my fork.

"Nope."

"You're so hetero, it's scary." I chewed then swallowed. "This is good."

"Thanks. I asked Becky for her recipe."

"When is she coming back from her brother's?"

"As soon as he's back on his feet. What kind of moron leaps off a roof? Oh! The game is on. Cool!" He sat up as if something amazing were playing on the TV. I gave the screen a peek, saw it was hockey, and rolled my eyes.

"That kind of person leaps off a roof," I snarked, waved at the hockey players, and then leaned up just as Hank had. "That's Tyr Hemmingsen," I whispered, sauce on my chin, as my eyes settled on the big man pummeling another big man. "Oh my God," I mumbled as the two combatants fell to the floor. Ice. It was ice. I felt my brother gaping at me then looked his way. "Yes, I know who he is."

"How?" he asked as the male people on TV were extolling the virtues of other male people in skates. It all sounded a little homoerotic to me. "You hate sports."

"I do, yes." I placed my plate on my knees and dabbed at the corner of my mouth with my pinkie finger. "He came into the club last night."

Hank's mouth fell open. It was kind of humorous. "Get the hell out of here."

I held up two fingers then frowned at my nails. They were such a mess. Prying fake nails off then gluing new ones on all the time was not good for healthy nails.

"He was. Scout's honor. Twice actually. Once with a group of other fisty type people, then by himself last night. He sat at that shady side table. You know the one." He shook his head. "Well, of course you do. Anyway, he sat there, his beret low, his shoulders high. The man was obviously trying to remain hidden."

"Wow, I never thought a guy like Tyr would go to Campo."

"It's not only gays that like drag, Henry." I snipped, then shoved more pasta into my face.

"No, hey, I know that. I love drag, it's just..." He shrugged. "Hockey players aren't normal straights."

"You'd know. Jocks of a feather and all that."

"I'm a good jock. The one's that gave you shit in middle school were asshole jocks. Lots of pro athletes are allies."

"Hmmm." I'd reserve commenting on that right now. I was sure some were, but on the whole, athletics and those who did them were bullies and gay bashers. This I also knew from firsthand experience. My attention lingered on the screen as the game began. "What number is Tyr, do you know?"

"Why do you want to know?"

"Just curious."

"Uh-huh. He's number forty-three."

"Thank you."

My brother streamed all kinds of sport. Anything that involved balls and men crunching other men and he was there. I sat on the edge of the sofa, eating my pasta, aghast at the physicality of this game. I knew it was rough. I'd seen some highlights here and there in my life. But watching it play out real time was just…jarring. And number forty-three seemed to be right in the middle of all the crunching. It was barbaric. I shook my head in wonderment.

"Is there a point to this game other than crunching people?"

"Checking. It's called checking. And yes, there is a point. You're supposed to put that puck into the net."

"And then you get a point?"

"Yes."

"So, if they're supposed to be trying to put the puck into the net, why are they bunched up in the corners crunching each other? What? It's a legitimate question."

"Checking. It's called checking and they're in the corners trying to free the puck. I need you to tell me about meeting Tyr Hemmingsen." I took another bite of my now cold food. I'd been hungrier than I realized. I tended to forget to eat when I was in dressmaking mode. "Did you talk to him?"

"I did. I even gave him a ride home. Oh! *Did you see that?!*" I leapt to my feet and pointed that the TV with my fork. "That man just crunched Tyr so hard, he flew over the side of the thingy and fell into the laps of the other team. Is that fair?!"

"Checking. It's called checking and yeah, that was a clean hit."

"I just cannot." I stalked off with my chilly pasta back to my sewing room. No. There was no way I could sit there and watch a sweet man like Tyr being crunched and bloodied. I had no clue what possessed a tender soul like Tyr to play such a violent sport, but he obviously had made a mistake when choosing his career path.

An hour passed and my dressmaking was not progressing well. Every time I heard the sport people on TV yelling, I got up, pretending to need something to drink or eat, and went to check on Tyr's health. I knew it was stupid, but the big lug had wormed his way under my skin.

"That's the fifth bottle of water you've taken into the sewing room in an hour. You'll be up pissing all night." Hank threw at me.

"I'm a thirsty bitch." I said, then lingered a bit, sipping water I didn't even want. "Are they winning?"

"Yeah, they are. The Warthogs look great so far. This is their year to win it all." Henry was such a sport person. I chewed on my ratty thumbnail for a moment as big men skated up and down the ice.

"Their color scheme is blasé."

Hank threw a scathing look back at me. "It's green and black. What's wrong with that?"

"Nothing, but the green has no pizazz." The camera moved from the ice where people were standing around, waiting for men in black and white to listen to music on headphones? Why was this part of the game? Were they going to break into a dance routine? Now *that* I could get into. Tyr's handsome face popped up. My water bottle sat on my lower lip. Oh, my garters. He was sweaty and panting, his basil-colored helmet sitting on his head. That really was a ghastly green. It leeched all the color out of his handsome face. "They should have gone with a bright parakeet green."

Hank snorted in amusement. "Send a text to the Warthog organization and tell them the uniforms need to be ebony and parakeet green."

"You're being a bitch. They'd love it. Maybe I'll mention it to Tyr the next time he shows up at the club and hides in the corners. We'll discuss color palates over cocktails." I sashayed back to my sewing room as my brother sputtered. It took me another hour to finally get to work properly. I kept rolling my chair from my pinning and cutting to steal peeks of the game. The Warthogs won. That made me happy for some bizarre reason I didn't want to poke at. Better to poke my finger than that.

Chapter Five

TYR

Waking up after a win always made the day brighter.

Or it usually did. This morning, I just felt out of sorts and couldn't put my finger on why. I could, though, put my hand on my rock-hard dick. Eyes drifting shut, the fantasy that had sprung to life after meeting Eli arrived right on time, just like a train. And imitating that train, it knocked me off my feet with its intensity. In my mind's eye, I saw him kneeling before me, his big brown eyes smoky, his pink lips stretched around my cock, his tiny hand cradling my balls. I blew apart in no time, my dick kicking like a mule as it spewed ropes of cum over my palm. Breathless from the intensity of that orgasm, I lay in bed, splayed out, huffing, sliding my slick palm down over my nuts until I found my hole. With a gasp, I slid two fingers in, riding out the lingering shivers of pleasure until my cock was flaccid. Only then did I pull my fingers free and open my eyes.

Words failed me. I was never a big word man anyway, but this wild, world altering attraction to a petite man with flaming red nails had me going in circles. Kind of like my Roomba Rosie when she found a really dirty spot on the carpet. That had been me since seeing Gigi that first night. I needed to stay away from that club and the man who performed there. There was just too much riding on me to let my desire for men become known. Perhaps after I was playing for the Mules, then I could come out. It would stir up all kinds of crap, but the pros would know how to handle it better. Yes, we had inclusivity training in the AHL. That had been implemented years ago from the kiddy leagues all the way to the NHL. And lots of players were proud allies. Despite all the training, there were still slurs heard on the ice and in the dressing room. Racial, homophobic, trans, and slams against women. I'd managed to keep a cool head when Ben, who was the worst on the Warthogs, began using "fag" as a put down. Dante usually stepped in to shame him into acceptable behavior, but he was simply saying aloud what many in the locker room felt. And so, I sat silently, chewing my tongue, and let the slams sink in deeper and deeper.

Kicking off the covers, I stalked into the bathroom to shower, my mood as dark as the morning. A cold rain pelted the windows of my apartment as I dressed for morning skate. Sipping an energy shake after I ate some eggs and fruit, I thumbed through social media. Somehow, I ended up on the Campo Royale page on Instagram. And there was Gigi, in all her glory, in an ad for a Halloween show next week. Tickets could be purchased online. I raced to the ticket site, paused for a moment, and then bought two. I would take Janine as a cover. As soon as the sale was finalized, a boulder of guilt dropped on me.

Taking Janine as my "date" to stare dreamily at the

man on stage was so wrong. It was incredibly shitty, yet I could not bring myself to cancel the order. I would just go to the Halloween show, then never again. Seeing Eli as Gigi would purge the lust from my system. A lust that I'd not felt since college and my crush on my roommate, Remy Larsen. God, he had been a beautiful man. Sleek and slim, a swimmer with a smile that melted my heart. He had been my first true crush and I'd worn my heart on my sleeve. Remy had noted my affection and distanced himself making sure to make his disgust clear. After that, I had sworn to myself that I would keep that gay side of Tyr deeply buried. And now, here I was, madly drawn to a drag queen, of all things.

"What is wrong with your head?" I asked my reflection in the window as I pulled on my coat. There was no reply from the transparent Tyr. The bus ride to the barn was a sullen one. I was drawn into myself, flogging my own spirit over and over for being so weak and for leading a nice girl like Janine on. The flagellation didn't stop even when I was on the ice an hour later. Dante had been saying something to me as we lingered along the boards shooting the shit. Morning skate was always pretty relaxed. Just a way to build on team bonding, as well as loosen up with some light drills. Lots of people were saying it was time to stop making players come in twice in one day when we could workout at home and study game tapes on our phones. Maybe its time had passed. Maybe not. Ben hated morning skate. Generally, because he was hungover. I didn't mind, but this morning, I was irritable with myself for being such a liar and so weak-willed.

"...asked me if she thought I would like it? I was like, baby, that is a fucking tentacle! Hell, no, I won't like it."

Dante laughed at his story. I chuckled along, even though I'd missed most of it. Then it happened. Ben skated up to us, smirking, and leaned on his stick.

"So, hey, this fag walks into a normal bar and—"

That was all of the tasteless joke he got out before my fist met his face. Later, when I was sitting in the head coach's office, I'd not even be able to recall hitting my teammate. Nor would I be able to recall leaping on him when he hit the ice and pummeling him around the head. The whole incident had been twenty seconds, tops, before Dante jerked me off Ben and slammed me into the boards, pinning me to the glass. It took all he had to hold me in place. My vision was scarlet. Ben was bleeding all over himself and the ice. It was bedlam for a few minutes.

"Jesus fucking Christ," Dante huffed as he escorted me from the ice with the defensive coach shouting at me at the top of his lungs. My hands were trembling, my knuckles torn and bloody from hitting Ben. My legs felt wobbly. Dante steered me down the chute toward the dressing room. "What the ever-loving fuck was that, Tyr?"

"I…it was…he called me a fag." I sagged against a wall, the rage that had overwhelmed me slowly dying back as the reality of what I had just done sank in.

"Dude, no he didn't. He was telling some sick joke." I blinked at my friend. He patted my shoulder. "Seriously, T, he never once mentioned your name. Is there anything that you want to tell me?" I shook my head then yanked my helmet off, jamming it under my arm as sweat ran into my eyes. I looked this way and that, Dante trying to keep his sight with mine, but I finally stared down at the floor. "Right, okay. But hey, can you look at me?" I lifted my eyes from my skates. "If there is ever *anything* that you need to tell me about anything, I will totally accept whatever that something may be. You and I are more than line mates. We're friends." He clapped a hand to the back of my sweaty neck then squeezed it. "Just know that no matter what, I will always stand beside you. Between you and me, Ben should have had a pop in the face a long time ago."

Staring into his eyes, I found no condemnation at all. Only friendship. Should I tell him about my secret? Would he really stick by me if he knew I liked men? Coach Lane came thundering down the corridor, gave me one dark look, then pointed at his office. Dante let go of my neck. And so, I went into the head coach's office and got royally ripped. Then I was benched for a game on top of the ass reaming. Ben, it turned out, was fine other than a broken tooth and a bloody nose.

"Now, before I let you go, I want to know if a slur was used on the ice." Coach's weary blue eyes bored into me. "Kelly said he heard Ben use the F word before you cleaned his clock. Is that true?"

"It was a joke." Fuck. I hated lying for a jerk like Ben, but I had to cover my ass. Attacking your teammate was not a good thing. Sure, tempers flared on occasion on a team. Players got mad at other players in the locker room. It happened. But I couldn't let myself react to gay jokes and slurs so strongly. People would start to suspect there was a reason I got so upset when certain words were used but not others.

"A pretty piss poor one," Coach said, then shoved his hands into his thinning hair. "Alright, this is the end of it, then. You sit out a game and Ben gets yet another hour of inclusivity training. If he uses any kind of objectionable verbiage again, do not hit the dumbass. Come to me."

"Yes, Coach. I'm sorry I lost my temper."

"It's what you do, War God." He slapped my shoulder then told me to get the hell out. I rose, nodded, and went to the dressing room. As much as it galled me, I needed to find Ben and apologize. I couldn't find him. Seemed he went to his dentist to get the tooth I'd chipped fixed. I sat at my cubicle, towel wrapped around my right hand, feeling as low as a man could feel. Dante tried to talk me out of my funk, but even his upbeat personality failed to lift me up. I thanked him for trying and went to find the head trainer to sew up the gash on my hand.

Tony Basso aka Phil *tsked* me repeatedly while tossing a few butterfly stiches across my knuckles.

"Between you, me, and the fence post, that punch in the face was long overdue," the short, squat man who looked so much like that satyr trainer in Disney's Hercules we'd named him Phil, whispered. "Last week, I was this close to doing it myself. He made some crack about dykes all being too ugly to get a man, so they turned to pussy. I got a niece who's a lesbian and it pissed me right off. Stop flexing your hand, you'll pop the stitches." I stopped flexing and stared at our trainer. "Rumor has it he said something about you being gay?"

"It was just a joke. I overreacted." Shit, I hated lying to cover Ben's ass.

"Yeah, sure it was." Phil wrapped some gauze around my hand. Then he looked right into my soul with aged gray eyes. "There's nothing wrong with being gay. Lots of people are."

"I'm not gay."

His lips flattened before quirking up into a sad smile. "Never said you were kid, just making an observation. Go home, take some Advil for the pain. You know the routine."

I certainly did. This wasn't the first time I'd been sewn up after a fight. It was, as Coach Lane had said, what I did. What the team and fans expected me to do, right after helping to score goals, that was. Everyone loved my grit. I got awards for it. Sometimes, though, I just wanted to be the Tyr that didn't wage war with everyone. In all honesty, that wasn't even what the war god of Norse legend was all about. He wasn't Ares. Tyr was concerned more with treaties and justice. But that was in the Old Norse world. Once the Vikings emerged, Tyr was pushed aside by Odin and Thor, who were more bloodthirsty. And so now, that was my role on the ice. The mad Viking god of war, Tyr, lover of battle, swords, and blood. But there was more to the god, just as there was more to me.

I went straight home after the confrontation with Ben and tried to reach out to him. He either had his phone off or wasn't accepting my texts/emails. The need to apologize sat in my belly like a smoldering chunk of lava. Guilt weighed down on me. I'd hit my teammate. Yes, it was warranted. In truth, someone should have punched Ben in the mouth years ago. But still, it was not my best moment. I wondered what my father would have thought of me acting like that and my shame grew.

I shuffled around my place for a few hours, watering plants, talking to Rosie my Roomba, and growing edgier and edgier. Dinner was takeout Chinese, which tasted bland and greasy. Burping eggroll, I pondered calling Janine to see if she would like to go out, but as I was staring at her profile on my phone, I was already halfway out the door to see Eli perform. Something was leading me to him. What that something was, I didn't dare to investigate for fear it was going to be yet another self-destructive moment. And it surely was. I knew it even as my boots hit the sidewalk. But if it was just one final time…

It would be fine. Just one last time. I'd hide in the shadows at the tiny table and sip Sprite. One last visit to hear his voice and see him in those gorgeous dresses.

Why I was so attracted to a man in a dress I could not begin to understand. Gigi was both a man and a woman, but also, she was neither. Or both. It was confusing the fuck out of me. I'd long known I was gay, way back when I was just sprouting facial hair, I'd known. I'd kept it well hidden, of course, still did, but I'd known. And it had always been men that drew my eye, never women. Until Gigi/Eli. Society laid out such strict rules. There were men and there were women. If you were a man who liked women, you were straight, if you were a man who liked men you were gay, if you were a man who liked both you were bisexual. Neat. Tidy. Until you brought drag queens into the equation. Then all the neat and tidy societal rules were blown out of the water.

Was I really attracted to women after all? Obviously, Gigi appealed to something in me, so was I really not gay? Was I bi or pan? Or did I need to stop letting the dictates of those tight gender rules hold sway over me? Drag, it seemed, didn't just challenge the rules of gender, it took that damned hammer of Thor's to them. Fucking Ben and his fucking gay jokes. Maybe the asshole should read something about the ancient gods before he spouted off about them. Expanding his mind would be a really good thing. The asshole.

The bus rumbled to a stop. I glanced out the window and there sat Campo Royale, red neon lips flashing. I rose to my boots and pushed out of the bus and into the club. Beret down to my eyebrows, I paid the lone man at the door and snuck inside, my goal that well-hidden table in the dark corner.

The server was the same girl that had been working last time. She gave me a quirky smile then placed a Sprite on the table before I even ordered.

"You tend to stick out, Big Guy." She walked off as I slunk a bit further into my seat. The first act was Monique Mason who told ribald jokes and danced to hip-hop tunes. I enjoyed her performance, even if the jokes were a little tawdry. Maybe my stupid joke level had been reached for the day. There was a break and tall, monotone Sitka took the stage. She was in a beaded caftan with a wig so orange it made my eyes ache. But she was funny. She made fun of herself, politicians, queers, straights, dogs, cats, no one was safe. As Sitka ran through her set, I peeked at the crowd. Lots of gay couples filled the tables. Everyone was so at peace with themselves. I longed for the luxury to simply be me.

The lights lowered. Everyone sat up a little straighter as Sitka announced Gigi. The screen behind the stage shifted from a billowy purple sort of graphic to what appeared to be an old nightclub. The image was black and white. There were palm trees in large clay pots, a piano, and little round tables with lamps and feathers in urns. It reminded me of the movie "Casablanca," in a way. Then, Gigi stepped into the lone white light.

My mouth went dry as I drank her in. She slowly walked to the microphone and I could not tear my eyes from her. She was wearing a watermelon pink gown with a slit that ran up to her hip. Each sultry step she took flashed a shapely leg in shimmering stockings. I even caught a peek of a garter belt, which made my cock throb. Her tiny feet were in white high heels which sparkled. My gaze swept up, taking in the hourglass figure—her waist was so small, my hands could span it with ease then lingered on her bare shoulders. They, too, sparkled as if she'd sprinkled diamond dust on her skin. Her makeup was perfect. Pink lips, rose tone eyeshadow, thick black lashes, and eyebrows that were slim yet bold. The wig she had chosen was red, pulled up on one side, the other side laying on her nude shoulder. My lungs felt hot. I took a deep breath, the first since she had appeared on stage.

"Hello, Campo Royale," she whispered into the microphone. The crowd went wild. My mouth dried up, but I was too smitten to take a drink. To hell with hydrating. I'd have to take my eyes from Gigi to find my drink. Her gaze moved over the room, then found me. I caught the small flicker of a perfect eyebrow before, "Are you all here to step back in time tonight?"

"We love you, Gigi!" some guy at the bar shouted. The other patrons laughed, as did Gigi.

"I love you, too," she replied with a tiny wave of a hand loaded with sparkling jewels. "How about we start my set off with a little something from the incomparable Peggy Lee?" Everyone clapped. Her gaze darted to me for a mere second and my skin caught fire. I wanted to shout something to her, to let her know that whatever song she sang would entrance me, but I merely gave my old tan beret a tug. Her lush lips twitched. She sang "They Can't Take That Away from Me" and I was lost to her voice and the music that filled the club. Her hour set was over far too quickly. I shot to my feet when she took her final bow, then realized that I was shouting and clapping. My cheeks got warm. I dropped back down into my seat and pulled my beret down to my nose, or close to it.

"Here, you look like you need something to cool you off," my server said as she placed a new glass of Sprite on a Club Royale coaster, then took my warm, flat one away. I peeked around my beret.

"Would you bring a—"

"Vodka and cranberry for the little lady?" I nodded as my ears burned. "Will do. I'll keep an eye out for Gigi, then bring it when she sits down with you."

"Thank you." I slipped her a twenty. "Keep the change."

She nodded, then gave the busy nightclub a quick onceover before her attention returned to me. "Look, Big Guy, I know she's a beauty, but she does not date fans. Ever. It's a rule for her and her house. So maybe you should set your sights on someone else?" I gaped at her. "Just trying to save you a broken heart."

"I...thank you." She sighed, then moved off to tend to her other customers. It was fine. My heart was safe. This would be the last time I was here, so there was no chance of my emotions being walked on. All I needed was this final time to talk with Eli. Maybe offer to take him home. Shit. I took the bus here. I'd call for a ride. It really was past time for me to buy a car. I lived too close to the rink that I didn't need it for work, and mass transit took me anywhere I needed to go. Dating would be easier, but the only person I dated was Janine and she…

"Is this seat taken?"

Gigi's sultry purr pulled me from my thoughts. I jumped up, smiling like a dolt, and pulled out the other chair for her. She'd changed from her watermelon dress into a feathery robe, this one pink as bubblegum. I felt silly being caught woolgathering.

"You changed faster this time," I offered as the sweet aroma of her floral perfume tickled my nose. I longed to bury my face in her neck so I could inhale the scent of roses and Eli. His masculine smell had to be there, lingering on his skin.

"I was curious," she answered, then sat back when her drink arrived. The server and the drag queen exchanged looks before the waitress hustled off to the bar. She took a delicate sip of her drink, sighed in pleasure, and turned those dark brown eyes to me.

"Oh?" I asked, sitting down across from her, my soda sitting untouched.

"Mm," she said around her straw, then placed her cocktail on a coaster. My sight lingered on the lipstick left behind on that straw. Steamy things began to percolate in my mind, making my dick swell quickly. "I'm curious about many things, when it comes to you. But my first question is, what happened here?" She tapped the white bandage wrapped tightly around my hand with a long, pink fingernail. I certainly didn't want to go into that shameful display, so I averted my gaze and mumbled something about a slash. "Honey, if her slash is *that* craggy, maybe you need keep your hand far away from it."

My gaze flew from my drink to her. "What? I…what?"

Gigi laughed lightly and I felt my heart flutter inside my chest.

"You're the type of man that makes a girl break all the rules," she said as her sight held mine.

I truly hoped so…

Chapter Six

ELI

WHAT THE EVER-LOVING FUCK ARE YOU DOING HERE, ELIJAH? Why are you flirting? This was supposed to be a simple kiki. Ask about his hand, then move on. Why are we making the cow eyes? Oh girl, you are so *going to get clocked!*

Honestly, my internal me talked as much as my external me and the bitch needed to shut it. Like, right now. This *was* a simple kiki. I just wanted to know about his bandages. We were friends. Well, not friends, but acquaintances. Masturbatory buddies. Did he tug one off while thinking of me? I certainly had been pounding my meat with visions of his sugarplums dancing in my head. The man was for the gods. Oh, shit, he *was* a god. Or named after one. No wonder my poor mortal eyes couldn't look away.

"So," I said to break the ghastly silence that had fallen over our little shadowy corner. "Did you like the show?" I leaned back in my chair and crossed one leg over the other, making sure that my sexy dressing robe slid open to show off my legs. Tyr's eyes dropped to my show of flesh and stayed there, his nostrils flaring. Oh, good God damn, my tuck was becoming incredibly uncomfortable. Pheromones wafted off the man, clouding my mind. I wanted nothing more than to take the massive brute home and fuck him silly.

He's straight. He has a girlfriend. Hussy bitch, just move on and talk to someone else before your ass gets—

"Oh, fuck off, you strumpet!" I spat. That brought those honey nut eyes of his from my legs to my face. "Not you, that bitch over there." I waved a hand in the air. He looked over his shoulder. "She's gone now." He opened his mouth to talk, then Sitka appeared. She made a pass of our table, her gaze lethal. I twisted to avoid her censorious look. "Oh, look, she's back. Ignore her." I tapped on the table with my fake nails to pull his attention from my drag mother. "So, a slash. Is that a hockey term?"

"It is. It means someone hits you with their stick. Why is she looking at me like she wants to hurt me?"

"Ignore her. Tell me more about hockey." He tried, bless him, but it grew harder and harder for him to focus when Sitka spent the next thirty minutes circling our table like a motherfucking great white. He seemed to be reluctant to talk about much of anything, so her trips back and forth were not helping. Every time I'd get him to open up a bit about his sport, she would pass by, sharp teeth bared as the theme from "Jaws" played in my head. Scooting this way and that on my chair to keep her spitting dark looks out of my visual didn't help. I was usually really good at blocking out unwanted glowers. I'd spent my whole life disregarding the venomous glares of the conservatives. Water and a duck's back, baby. But when those stink eyes came from mother dearest, they were much harder to brush off.

"…Halloween?"

I snapped back to the sexy bastard in the ugly beret staring at me. "I'm sorry. What about Halloween?"

"I saw the ad for the show. Will you be in it?"

"Yes, I'm one of the headliners." Sitka roamed by. We exchanged visual volleys, then I zeroed in on Tyr, he of the plump lips and killer thighs. I bet he could crush me between them. My dick was so hard now, no gaff was going to hide it. "I've just about got it done. Would you like to see it?" His gaze lingered on my face, a hundred emotions playing out in those beautiful eyes of his.

Elijah Benton McBride, what the fuck, henny? Why are we inviting the straight man with the girlfriend back to our house?!

I slapped the shade out of my internal Eli and waited. And waited. And waited. Maybe Internal Eli was right. No matter how much my dick wanted into this man's bubble butt, he was obviously working through something with his sexuality. Then, there was that leggy blonde who had had her ass tight to his crotch that night. Still, when he softly nodded, all thoughts of blonde bitches and uptight drag mothers went right out the window.

"Perfect. Give me thirty to put Gigi back in her bottles. Can you chill for that long?"

"Yeah, I have all night. I'm not playing tomorrow." He looked really sad about that. Was it due to the slash thing? Or was it not his night to play? What did I know? Well, I knew I wanted to get the fuck out of here. Sitka was boring holes into me.

"Good. Sip on your soda for half an hour, then we'll go see my dress."

He rose when I did. It was ridiculously sweet. I swept past Peggy, the server for this side of the floor tonight. She'd also been tossing some shade my way with cutting looks. Honestly, was this whole club filled with nothing other than shady whores? Well, duh. We *were* all drag queens. Still, now the servers were knocking on the library doors? Not tonight. I was not about to be read this evening. This morning. Whatever.

No sooner was I inside my closet when Sitka came blasting in like a fucking winter storm.

"Gigi," she said, then flung the door closed right in Monique's nosy pug face. Sorry, that was a nasty slam on pugs, who are adorable poochies. Still, when the pug fits…

"Just hold onto your library card," I tossed over my shoulder as I removed my good gown to keep it clean. My dry-cleaning costs were astronomical. "You're not reading me tonight."

She stomped up behind me, her long face set tightly. "Elijah, you're thinking with your cock."

The fact that she was using my real name instead of my drag name while I was in drag spoke to how upset she was.

"Please." I huffed, then glanced down at my crotch. Oh. "It's not a date. It's a one-night fling." She rolled her eyes. I spun from her disapproval to sit down and start removing layers of makeup.

"Where have I heard that before." She moved to stand behind me, her hands coming to rest on my shoulders. I loved the shade of polish she was wearing but I was not going to tell her. There. Take that. "Eli, my sweet cucumber." Now it was time to roll my eyes. "You know the rules are there for our protection."

"I know. And they're good rules. I have no plans to date the man. Just fuck him. Several times." She flicked my ear. "Ouch!"

"Eli, baby, this has heartache written all over it." She rubbed my shoulders. I kept my sight on my own face in the mirror. "I know what I'm talking about."

"I know you do. And I know what I'm doing. Dating fans is forbidden. Fucking fans is not." I tugged a wipe free to remove the cold cream.

"That works only for the bitches who can separate sex from love."

I frowned. "I can do that." She said nothing. I flung my wipe to the floor. "*I can!* My dick is no longer a direct route to my heart." She did not look convinced. "Honestly, it's fine. He's probably just a curious straight boy. I'll satisfy his curiosity. We both get off and he goes home. See, it's all perfectly good. Now go piss on some other Patel child's parade."

Her fingers bit into my shoulders as her lips pressed together. Then, with a sigh worthy of an Oscar nomination, she bent down to kiss my sweaty hair.

"Very well, my precious piddly, but don't pretend you weren't warned. I've seen the way he looks at you. If you think you'll walk away from this unscathed, you're not the clever child I thought you were."

With that, she exited as regally as the queen she was. I whipped another wipe to the floor, huffed, bent down to pick it and the other one up, then flung them into my tiny little pink trash can. Sitka was worrying needlessly. One quick round of hide the wienie and poof! This clawing urge to dream about one big, dumb jock would evaporate. I'd work him out of my system and that would be that.

He'd go back to his woman and his jock life and I'd continue my climb to the top of my profession. I had my eyes on the prize. Ms. Queer America. Oh, yes, I so wanted that crown. Then, my name would have some real weight. Someday RuPaul would send *me* tickets to fly out to LA and be on her TV show. Then, I'd be known all over the country and not just on the east coast. Until then, it was all about busting ass and travelling. Building the fan base. Winning as many pageants as I could.

With my head on straight—or as straight as a gay man in a fucking corset would get his head—I shimmied into my street clothes. A thick teal sweater, skinny jeans, and a fluffy chartreuse coat with big silver buttons. Oh, and my purse. A snappy clutch. Purse first, bitches, to quote Bob the Drag Queen. Arm extended, purse leading the way, I sashayed up to Tyr, who had seen me coming and got to his feet. What a polite pumpkin he was.

"Eli's back," I teased, tapping his bulky bicep with my purse. "Did you miss him?"

"Yes." The gag was real. Stunned at his honesty, I simply stood there and stared up at him.

"Follow the purse." I grabbed his wrist and pulled him along behind me, right past the bar where Monique, Sitka, and Clarise were all watching. Chin high, I tugged Tyr out the front door and took a deep breath of chilly air. God, that was a gauntlet of shade right there. My phone was about to blow the fuck up. Whatever. I'd sort through all the worrisome shit on the morrow. Right now, I had other things on my mind. I hoped Tyr Hemmingsen was prepared for the ton of gay sex that was about to drop down on his oh-so broad shoulders. And dick. Don't forget the dick.

TYR WAS quiet on the ride home. He seemed the stoic sort, which turned me right the hell on. Turned me on more I should say. But it was fine. I talked enough for both of us. I wasn't even sure of what I'd told him as our driver carted us to the lower-to-middle class house Hank and I called home. Other than telling him about my brother and I sharing the place and how much I loved Scottish romance novels, hot tea with spearmint, and poodle dogs. I *really* loved curly poodle dogs. He smiled at me the whole while. How I kept my ass in my seat and didn't climb him like the mighty Danish oak he was—did they even have oak trees in Denmark—was only due to the old lady behind the wheel. She was, no joke, a hundred if she were a day. Yet she was rocking some dank tunes from Kendrick Lamar.

"Welcome to the House of McBride," I announced as I threw open the front door. "My brother Hank is working, so you won't be roasted about sport while you're here." I took his massive hand in mine, then led him down the short hall quickly so he couldn't focus on our second-hand furnishings too closely. He probably had cash to burn, being an athlete. I pulled him to my sewing room. "And in there is where Gigi is gowned, coiffed, and otherwise made stunning."

I flipped on the light. He ducked a bit to clear the doorjamb then instantly removed his beret. His hair was thick, flat from the beret, of course, but still wavy in spots. It needed a fluff. My fingers itched to be the fluffer. Instead of being a radically slutty Sue, I shed my coat, dropped it and my purse to the floor, and began prancing around the room. His eyes followed me, then darted to the piles of breastplates, padding, and wigs stashed into every corner and cranny. My shoes and boots literally were flowing out of the overstuffed closet. The poor man seemed slightly overwhelmed with it all. Hell, sometimes the sheer magnitude of crap it took to be Gigi overpowered me, as well. When that happened, I'd just go buy some new pumps and the feeling went away.

"This is my Halloween dress. Do you love it?!" I pushed the sewing form from the corner to the middle of the room. I kicked a pair of shears out of the way, then centered it right in front of him. "I can tell you adore it."

"It's beautiful." He touched the bodice as if there were a breast nestled in it. "And you sewed this?" My head bobbed with pride. "That's incredible. This dress is…I bet it looks wonderful on you."

"Oh, it does!" I winked and got another gruff snort of a laugh that went right to my balls.

"I hope I can see you in it."

"Come to the show. I'll get you and your girl tickets."

His playful side disappeared. "She's not my girl."

Huh. "Has anyone told *her* that?"

"She's just a person that I date when…when I need a date."

Ahh. Okay. Yep. My gaydar was not off then. He *was* queer, just hiding behind a beard. Which, given what he did for a living, made sense. What was it that Sitka had said?

Don't get involved with fans?

No bitch, the other thing. We're not getting involved, we're merely fucking.

Delusional much, hunty? As if you ever just fuck and move on.

We're not doing this right now, because hello!? Stud alert. Focus on the thing that Sitka said. About professional sports, bastions, and repressed homo boys.

Oh, that. Yes, let's just focus on that little tidbit but ignore the motherfucking Viking standing in the room fingering your stuff.

That man can finger anything I own.

I give up.

"Uh-huh. Oh-kay, well, do you want a ticket for the girl you date when you need a date?"

"No. I already have a ticket."

"Impatient much?" I teased and got a ruddy blush to tint his cheeks. "Seriously, I will get you tickets if you want."

"I probably shouldn't have bought them though," he commented as his sight flickered to me.

"There's no law against going to a club, Tyr Hemmingsen." That was a little tart. I worked up a smile to counter the bitterness. "Bring a friend."

He nodded. "Okay, yeah, that's…okay. I'll bring a friend. Thank you."

Ugh. If he brought that blonde, I might hurl.

We're just fucking. Did you forget?

No, Madame Cow, I did not forget. I hope he brings her. She seems nice. There. Bitch.

"So, these are my stage costumes," I announced with a bit more nervous energy evident than a casual fuck should be projecting. "All hand sewn. Thank you." I cut a deep curtsy. Tyr chuckled. It was a rumbly sound from deep in his chest. My dick purred in delight. He moved slowly around the chaotic room, carefully placing his huge Red Wing boots to avoid stepping on material tossed to the floor and every other surface. He ran the tips of his fingers along the flowing gowns and tea dresses, his face soft and appreciative. "That wall over there holds all my wigs."

He threw a look at the shelves. They were packed full. "Do you fix the wigs yourself too?"

"Of course. It's all part of being a killer queen."

"I got that reference." He flashed me a smile as he toyed with the sleeves of a dark blue evening gown with silver beading. "Sometimes, I think you're speaking a different language."

A small giggle burbled up out of me. "Drag is a world unto itself, lamb."

His sight darted from the dress he was caressing to me. "Lamb?"

"Mmhmm." I nodded as I tapped my chin. "Do you mind if I call you that?"

"No, I suppose not." He lifted the hem of a gossamer pearly white gown and held it to his nose. His lashes dropped down as he breathed. When his eyes opened, his pupils were blown. "They all smell like roses. Just like you."

For the life of me, I cannot say what it was that came over me in that moment. Perhaps it was just pure lust. The man *was* gorge. Perhaps it was something a little deeper. He knew my scent. Maybe it was Satan. Whatever or whoever caused it, I launched myself at him. He gasped when my arms snaked around his neck, but he didn't fight at all when my mouth crashed over his. There was a millisecond of shock on his part, then he got fully into the program. His tongue met mine at the same time his hands found my ass. He lifted me from the floor as if I were a bag of feathers. My legs went around his middle. Tongues tangled. His fingers dug into my ass. My ratty nails pressed into the back of his neck. The kiss went on and on, his tongue filled my mouth, roaming over my teeth then retreating so that I could tongue fuck him. A low thrumming sound vibrated through him and into me.

"Fuck, oh fuck," I gasped when the kiss broke. He buried his face in my neck, then took a step or two, his teeth raking over my jugular. I grabbed at his head. And then we were at the fainting couch, his body coming down over top of mine. Still, I clung to him, desperate to keep him close, to feel that thick ridge of his arousal as it settled next to mine.

"I want you," he mouthed into my throat as his thick thigh slid between my legs. I gasped, arched, and clawed. He growled like a panther, his ass rolling in deep round motions that drove all rational thought from my head.

"Fuck yes. I want to suck you then ride you until we go blind."

He huffed, pumped his hips, and found my mouth again. We suckled and nipped at each other's mouths, our gyrations growing hotter, my cock aching with need. God, he tasted divine. Like lemon-lime soda and destiny. I needed more. I needed his prick in my mouth, in my ass.

"Off, off," I panted beside his ear. He drew back to stare down at me with lust-hazed eyes. "I want to suck your cock." I shoved lightly. He moved just enough to ease his weight off me. I missed it immediately. "Mm, yes," I scrabbled around until I was on his lap, his face between my hands. I gave him a wicked smile that he returned with a shaken, wobbly look. Then, I licked into his mouth. His hands roamed under my sweater, rough fingertips rolling along the bumps of my spine. His cock lay next to mine. I nibbled at his lips, then his chin. He tugged my top off, then ran his palms over my sides and chest, flicking my nipples, then lifting my arms high over my head.

"You're smooth as a rose petal," he said, his voice gruff with passion. Then, he pressed a kiss to my hairless arm pit. I snorted and twitched. He smiled up at me, then licked the sensitive skin. A moan rolled out of me.

"How is a man who beats up other people for a living so damn poetic?" I asked, not expecting a reply as his face was buried in my arm pit.

"My mother was a poet," he murmured, then moved to the other arm pit, laving the skin, taking a small bit between his lips to suck a mark on my skin. "You're so beautiful. So manly and yet so feminine. My head is...I want you."

"Oh, you have me, honey." I wiggled free of his grip, kissed him hard, and then peeled off his shirt. He was my polar opposite. Where I was hairless, he was hairy. I rubbed my hands over his pecs, loving the way the crisp brown curls moved over my fingers. "I love big, hairy men."

"Lucky me." His fingers skipped over my ribs, up and down, up and down.

"You have no idea just how lucky. I'm breaking one of Mother's prime directives." He looked at me in confusion. "Not important. Totally worth the weeks of upcoming parental lectures."

With that, I shimmied down to the floor. He spread his magnificent thighs for me. My gaze stayed tangled with his as I tugged down his zipper to free his cock. The slick head peeked at me from the top of his underwear. I nearly came right then and there. I was a bit of a size queen, as well as being a drag queen. Gigi loved all the crowns. I jerked his briefs down under his balls, sighing at the sight of two massive hairy nuts, then licked a stripe up from his sac to the tip of his head. The salty taste of precum coated my tongue. God, he tasted fantastic.

"I hope you have a strong heart, baby," I whispered. His eyes flared. I swallowed him down. Oh yes, he was never going to forget this night. I would make sure of that.

Chapter Seven

TYR

I HOPED I DID, AS WELL.

This man was going to kill me, and I found that I didn't care one bit if I passed away tonight. At least my time would come making love to a man. I'd move over to the great beyond being me. The real me.

"I think it…God, Eli," I coughed out as he took every bit of me into his mouth. He hummed as my dick filled his throat. My balls tightened up. "Close…shit!"

He pulled off with a pop, his tongue lingering on the head, the pink tip delving into my slit. His hand grasped my cock at the base, squeezing hard, as I clung to what little control I had. Which wasn't much. In all honesty, I'd not had any control over much of anything since the first time I'd seen Gigi on stage. Now, I was at the mercies of the Norns, as were all men and gods. Urd, Verdandi, and Skuld were casting lots with my fate carved on them. Perhaps they might toss them down the well, beside their lodge under Yggdrasil.

"Thinking about hockey stats?" Eli enquired, his lips sliding down over my engorged head.

"Norse…mythos…fate…it's been so long." I thrust upward, my heels on the floor, pattern paper crunching and sliding under my pumps.

"Do you want to come down my throat or in my ass?" A groan rolled out of me unbidden.

"Both," I huffed, grabbing the arm of the petite sofa that I was sitting on.

He shuddered wantonly. "That was no help. I want you in my ass."

"You're bossy for such a little thing," I commented, watching with fascination as he stood up, then peeled his pants and thong off in one swift movement. His cock bounced up to smack his belly. His balls were bare. There wasn't a hair to be seen anywhere.

"You'll learn to love it." He bent over, found his purse, and dug into it as my eyes roamed over his shapely legs then back up to his prick. It was long and curved upward. I longed to take it into my mouth. I'd never done that for a man. The one lover I'd had in college was…well, it was dark, we were drunk, and it wasn't a great experience for either of us. He'd wanted to fuck me but came all over my ass before he even penetrated me. Which was probably for the best, because as soon as he blew a nut, he threw up on my back. Not a good experience at all.

"I think I will," I replied without thinking. If I'd been rational, I'd have said "No, I won't learn to love it because this cannot ever happen again." But I wasn't rational at all. I was acting in ways that were dangerous to my career. Yet, when he pulled out a ribbon of condoms and packets of lube, all care for the future dissipated. There was nothing beyond this moment and the beauty of this tiny firebrand of a man.

"Get this on," he tossed me a condom. I fumbled terribly with rolling it on my dick. It was impossible to keep my eyes on condom placement when he was working lube up into his ass. His eyes were at half-mast, his head back exposing his swanlike neck, and his mouth was in a perfect pink O that made my nuts tingle. "Mm, fuck, I need something bigger than my fingers."

His dark eyes dropped to my cock. "Will this do?" I grabbed my cock and shook it.

"That will do nicely." He climbed onto the padded bench thing, one leg on either side of me, and squatted over my cock, his tongue darting out to dampen his lips. "Hold your cock still. That's perfect, lamb. Perfect." His gaze met mine. "You let me do all the work, okay?"

"Yes…yes…" I held my cock tightly. He sat down slowly, lowering himself down onto me inch by hot, slick inch. My eyes rolled to the back of my skull. Eli took me all. Every inch of me was buried in his body. I held him with my left hand, my right releasing my dick when he was seated on me to find the arm of the sofa. "Tight…Eli… you're tight." I lifted my head to look at him.

"Mm, lamb, that's because you're so fucking big." He sat still for a moment, his lower lip between his teeth, his eyes squeezed shut. "I love the burn of a big cock stretching my ass. Do you bottom?"

"Yes, anything…with you, anything."

His lips twitched, then he leaned in to kiss me, his tongue sliding over and around mine. I pumped up. He sucked in a sharp breath.

"Sorry, I just need…" I nibbled at his chin, the arm of the tiny sofa cracking as I jerked on it to regain my footing.

"I know what you need." He then tucked his knees tightly to my hips and began moving up and down, side-to-side, and round and round. "How's that? Ah…Jesus, you're huge. Fuck. Oh, fuck I…yes!" He cried out when I pinched a pink nipple.

So, I took them both and rolled them. He began riding me harder, then, his ass slapping my thighs, his cock bouncing and dropping droplets of precum on my belly. I pinched his left nipple, then reached for his dick. He threw his head back and came all over my chest. Spunk flew all over as he pulsed and pounded his ass on my cock. That tight channel of his convulsed and I was done. I thrust up with all I had, lifting my ass from the sofa. Eli yelped. More cum burst out of him, dotting my chin and eyelashes. He bounced up and down with vigor, madly milking me out. I jerked and pumped into him, unable to form words. I merely grunted and groaned. His mouth slammed down over mine, his hands grabbing handfuls of hair as we rode out our orgasms.

Eli melted like a crayon in the sun. He fell onto my chest, his nose resting against my neck. I released the now slightly wobbly arm of his loveseat sofa thing to run my fingers up and down his sweaty back. I felt him tighten around me. A shiver of pleasure coursed through me. I pressed a kiss to his silly blue hair then sighed, the afterglow of making love to a man settling on me like a warm blanket on a cold day.

He wiggled his skinny ass with a moan. I grabbed a tiny buttock, then nosed at his ear until he lifted his head. His eyes were soft and sweet, sleepy from sex. I wanted to kiss him. He read my mind, it seemed, for he pressed his puffy lips to mine. Keeping my hand cupped to his ass, we made out leisurely, the moment a tender one leaving me searching for what to say.

"You're the most incredible thing," I finally went with, which was stupid, dorky, and not at all what I should be saying. The ugly fingerlings of reality began to wiggle in, scratching away the veneer of tenderness and affection that had taken root in my heart.

"You're not too shabby, yourself," he replied, then slowly lifted his heat from me. Which was...yeah, sure, it was time, but I hated the cold air rushing over me. I wanted him back, warming me, kissing my jaw, whispering sweet things that lovers whisper. Only we weren't lovers. Nor could we ever be. I sat up as he got to his feet, my cock still hard within the condom. "You have cum on your eyelashes."

He grinned and used his thumb to clear the thick drop. I reached for him, easing him closer, then pushing my face into the concave of his stomach. Roses. His skin still smelled like them, even after sex. Closing my eyes, I drew his scent deep into my lungs.

"I don't want to go," I whispered into his soft skin. His hand came to my head, his nails making soft little tracks along my skull. He said nothing as I held him. When I realized how immature I sounded, I released the man, then pulled out the mask of the war god that I wore. It felt like a witch's brindle as it kept me from speaking the truth. "Sorry, that was not cool."

"No, hey." He captured my chin, then tipped my head back. I tried to stay free of the pull of his gaze, but it was no use. I fell headlong into his eyes. "It was totally cool. I don't want you to go, either. Why don't we get washed up and see what happens?"

That lifted my spirits. Surely, it would be okay to spend a few more hours with Eli. After all, this was the last time. I nodded. He smiled and kissed my mouth. We padded around picking up our clothes then went to his bedroom. It was just as chaotic as his sewing room. He found some wipes and cleaned me up, rising to his toes to clean his spunk from my face. I slid my arm round his middle then lowered my mouth to his. I could kiss him all night. He sighed into the kiss, then broke free, taking me to his bed. I removed and tied off the condom, dropping it into the full trash can beside his bed. He flung clothes, books, and shoes to the floor, crawled under the covers, then stretched out.

"Come cuddle for a little while," he softly said.

There was no way I could say no, so I joined him under the covers. The bed smelled of roses and Eli. He curled into me, then over me, his lips and teeth exploring my body. We were soon hard again. He climbed atop me, took our cocks in his tiny hand, and got us both off. He was still shuddering from his release when I rolled him to his back to taste his mouth. I was like a man who'd been imprisoned and only fed stale bread for years. Eli was my buffet.

"God, you're insatiable," he gasped, when I went down on him a few minutes later. His cock was soft but slowly swelled as I clumsily sucked on it. He fucked my mouth, his release taking forever, but what did I care? This night could go on for an eternity, as far as I was concerned. My chin was coated with spittle and spunk when he was done. He pulled me up over him, kissed his way into my mouth to lap up his spunk on my tongue. "You want my ass again?"

"Yes, gods, yes," I whimpered. He rolled to his belly after pulling a dirty shirt from the floor to lay under him as I booted up. I touched his hole, fascinated at its frilly exterior. He whined and cooed as I worked slick into him. Eli demanded two fingers, then three, and then my cock. I pushed into him, my latex-covered dick going deep. This joining was slower but just as magnificent. He pushed back with each of my thrusts, grunting and digging at the bedding. I came so hard, my head spun. He followed along quickly, his fist working his cock.

Unable to move more than an inch or two, I teetered to the side and collapsed beside Eli on the bed. He made small little sounds as he moved to his side, using an old Army t-shirt to wipe his hand clean. He lobbed the camo shirt toward the corner of the room. It almost hit the hamper but fell short.

"You're a slob," I murmured as he snuggled in tight to my side. I glanced at the small clock on his dresser. Nearly five in the morning. Making love all night ate up the time.

"You're hairy," he replied, then peppered my bicep with tiny kisses. "And amazing."

That made me smile. He pulled the covers up over us then let his cheek rest on my chest.

"You're pretty amazing, too," I whispered, which got me a sweet coo of appreciation.

My eyelids were getting heavy. I was warm, sated, and had Eli beside me. There was no rush to get up and dressed. Fuck that mask of shame. I'd just lie here with him for a little bit longer.

MY PHONE ALARM WENT OFF, jarring me from that misty place between sleep and wakefulness. I never sleep well in a strange place, so I'd been on the cusp anyway. Eli had moved to his side during the past hour or so, his head nearly obscured with blankets. Disturbing him felt wrong. What was the point? Might as well leave and make the cut a clean one. So, I didn't touch him other than to take a strand of turquoise hair between my fingers and rub it. Then, I slid out of the bed, found my pants, and turned off my alarm. A run this morning was out. Hell, I'd sweated enough making love to Eli to skip a jog. I'd head home, shower, and go to the barn.

There, I could apologize to Ben and try to get my life back on track. I searched high and low for my underwear but came up empty, so I jumped into my jeans commando and finished dressing. Not wanting to be a total dick, I fished around for a pen and slip of paper under the bed, finding a Bic and a receipt for a fabric shop purchase. I scribbled a note to Eli, thanking him for a wonderful night and telling him that I would never forget him. I placed it on his dresser and put a bottle of perfume, rose water, on top of it.

At the door, I paused to stare at the little form under the heavy blankets. I felt the ties that were already forming between us tightening. It would be so nice to simply stay. But that was out of the question. I'd taken enough chances going to Campo Royale twice. It was imperative that no one suspect I was gay. I had to get to the pros. I turned the knob, stepped out into the dimly lit hall, and came face to face with a man in a blue uniform who looked so much like Eli it had to be his brother. Bigger by far, but the same eyes, nose, and chin.

We both jumped.

"*Jesus!*" Hank yelped, his eyes wide, then narrowing as he made the connection. I could see the cogs falling into place and cursed myself for being such a weak man. "Tyr Hemmingsen? Holy shit, it is you! Holy shit! Wow. I'm like…wow."

The door behind me swung open and Eli padded into the hall, hair on end, naked as the day he was born, my briefs dangling off his index finger. I could hear my professional career being flushed down the toilet. Hank's gaze went round as dinner plates as he took in his brother's rumpled appearance, the beard burns on his whole body, as well as the several vibrant hickeys dotting Eli's skin. If there were a hole in the ground, I would have crawled into it.

"Holy shit, are you gay?" Hank asked me. I didn't know where to go or what to say. So, I stood there slack-faced. "Holy shit, you *are* gay. And just nailed my baby brother!"

"Three times," Eli added, then began twirling my underwear on his finger.

"Three times?" Hank gasped, then looked at me with what appeared to be admiration. I simply wanted to die. Right here in the hallway. Death, take me now.

"This is not the right thing to be discussing with your brother," I finally coughed out and snagged my briefs from his finger.

"Why not? Are you ashamed?" Eli enquired.

"No, of course not. I'm just…I'm not…maybe a little!" I spat back.

"You could have at least said goodbye, is all I'm saying," Eli sniped, his hurt face morphing into an expression of confusion. Hank folded his arms over his chest and listened.

"I left a note on your dresser," I explained, wondering why Hank was so amused by all of this.

"Oh, *please*!"

"I did. It's under the rose water," I argued.

"I'm caught in this really weird place between wanting to leave because this is personal, yet I kind of want to stay to hear this because it's personal. Also, dude, you're gay?!" Hank asked for about the tenth time.

"Yes, he is gay. Oh my God, Henry Jones! He's gay. Queer as a football bat, okay? Can you move past it?!" Eli snapped, before storming back into his room. Hopefully to find clothes to cover his love marks. I felt sick to my stomach.

"Sorry, I didn't mean to…" Hank rubbed at the nape of his neck. "I just never assumed…never heard a thing about you being gay."

"I'm not…" I almost denied it. That was my default. But there was really no sense in denying it now. I'd been caught red-handed sneaking out of a man's bedroom with his cum dried in my hair. Shit. My hair must be a sight. Where was my beret? Dammit. It was in Eli's room somewhere. Could this night—morning—get any worse? "I'm not out."

Hank nodded thoughtfully. "Wow, this is just…Nope, it's not anything. It's cool. Really cool. I'm really stoked that you're being gay with my brother."

"*Oh my gods, Henry! Stop!*" Eli's shout leaked around the door.

Henry grimaced. "Sorry, I just never expected to run into the War God of Wilmington exiting my brother's room at the ass crack of dawn."

"Please, do not tell anyone. If this got out, it could ruin my chances at making it into the pros." The begging tone in my voice didn't sit well, but if I had to grovel to keep this secret, I would. I was so close to the goals my father had dreamed of for me. To see it all come crashing down because of who I took to bed would be devastating.

"Oh, no worries. Your secret's safe with me." Hank smiled, crossed his heart, then cracked me on the shoulder with a brotherly swat. "So, are you and Eli dating now?"

The door to my back flew open with force. Eli stormed out, shouldered his way between us, shoved my beret into my chest, and stalked down the hallway, his pink and black feathered robe billowing out behind him.

"He's mad," Hank whispered. I nodded before pulling my beret onto my head. I wished it were a ski mask. "Hey, if you two are dating—"

"We are not dating. I don't date fans," Eli shouted from some other part of the house, the front door, I discovered, after Hank slunk to his room and I bumbled down the hall to the living room. I shuffled to the door, hat on my head, underwear in my back pocket. Eli opened the door, admitting a rush of brisk fall air into the old house. He shuddered, then pulled his thin robe tighter around his middle. "You should go before the neighbors all wake up."

I glanced out the door at the house across the street. He was right. I should go and never return.

"I'm sorry."

"Don't be sorry. I found the note. It was sweet. You're

sweet. I wish…" He blew a wisp of blue hair from his brow. "I wish a lot of things."

"Me, too."

He rose to his bare toes, kissed me on the mouth, and then tried to push me out the door. "Go, before Mr. Wright next door wakes up and comes out to get his paper to see you running for the bus."

"I'll call for an Uber."

He shook his head, but his lips were twisted up in a smile. "Yeah, I wish. Go, before I lure you back to my bed for round four. Not that my ass could take another pounding, but yours is untouched." He winked and my dick twitched. This man had enchanted me. It was magic. It had to be. I bent down to peck his cheek then I backed away, out into the cold dawn.

"Goodbye, Eli," I said.

"Goodbye, Tyr."

He closed the door in my face and turned off the porch light. I glanced skyward as my heart thudded feebly in my chest.

It was for the best.

It was for the best.

Maybe if I kept telling myself that, I'd believe it someday.

Chapter Eight

ELI

THE FOLLOWING WEEK SUCKED.

Wait. Suck isn't strong enough. Sometimes sucking can be fun. Like when you have a fat, hard Danish cock pressing on your tonsils and—

Fuck me with a cactus dipped in kerosene. That was one of the biggest reasons for the seven hideous days after the one fabulous night. Tyr. He had taken up residence in my head. And in my heart. Yes, fucking sue me, I had fallen for the man. Sitka had called it. She knew that I couldn't offer up my body without stapling my stupid fickle heart to it. UGH! What was my problem?! Why couldn't I do one-night stands like every other cross-dressing whore I knew? Speaking of cross-dressing whores…

Monique was reason number two this week had been unspeakable filth. I have no proof of her involvement, but I was sure that she was the reason the pipes running across the ceiling of my dressing cupboard had burst on Wednesday night. With the closet soaking wet, along with several of my stage dresses, four wigs, and two pairs of beaded shoes, I was forced back into general population. Monique gloated nonstop while I was carrying all my possessions back to the main dressing room.

"Well, look what the toiled flushed out," Monique cackled as I passed with the final armload of hip pads. "Maybe that burst pipe did you a favor and washed all that drug store make-up of yours down the drain."

Clarice bumped into me; I had hit the brakes in such a hurry. All six girls in the dressing room twisted their heads like owls to watch two drag queens throw some shade. And maybe a stiletto.

"Bitch, please, you know I only order from Judith Waverly in Manhattan, which is why you steal my lipstick all the time." The girls all snapped their fingers in appreciation of the slam.

"Okay, girls, enough," Clarice said with authority. "Let's save the kitty shit for later. You sit here next to Jo-Jo, Gigi."

"Wasn't that the name of the that puppet from that old TV show?" Jo-Jo, a chunky girl from Jersey with a heart of gold, piped up. Honestly, Jo-Jo Jewels was the Campo Royale Miss Congeniality. Maybe sitting beside her would rub off. Fuck knows I'd been a miserable twat for days now.

"No, tiddles, that was Topo Gigio," Sitka announced, before dropping a box of wet wigs at my tiny feet. "And the show was Ed Sullivan. Fuck *all* you bitches for the saggy queen comments bursting to life on your tongues."

"At least it's just a comment on my tongue. Rumor has it that Monique has thrush," Jo-Jo tossed into the air.

"Well, that makes two parts of her that are yeasty. Her mouth and her pussy!" I batted it over the fence.

We all roared. Well, all of us other than Monique. Bitch never could take a joke. Hell, even Sitka laughed. Monique stalked off on her dollar store heels.

"When she claims that her pussy is on fire, girl, she is not lying!" Clarice chimed in and we had another good laugh. Nothing could beat the catty level of a room full of flaming fluffs who called themselves drag queens.

Sitka chuckled in that chain-smoker huff of hers before exiting GP to call a plumber. As much as I loathed Monique, it was nice to be here with the girls. They all hated her skinny ass, too. My somewhat good mood evaporated when I looked down into the box of soaking wet wigs at my feet. Ugh. I had to tend to them, or they'd be musty come morning.

So that was why I went home and was shampooing, conditioning, detangling, and then setting synthetic wigs instead of getting ready for reason number three this week kept getting worser and worser.

"Hey," Becky called from the doorway of my sewing room. I craned my head, curlers in my hand and bobby pins between my lips, to look her way. She smiled and some of the crankiness left my soul. Some. Not all. Becky Smith—I swear on my grandmother's girdle that is her real name—was everything that was sunshine and motherfucking lollipops. No, shit. My brother was dating frigging Sleeping Beauty. Dark haired, bright eyed, sweet, chipper. I had no doubts Becky had all the woodland animals in Wilmington coming to her little house to help her with chores. I loved her to bits. How my dopey-ass jock brother had landed a darling button like her, I would never know. "Are you going to be ready soon?"

I sighed. She frowned a bit, then stepped into the madness that was my room. Her little feet stepped over the flotsam covering the floor. She was dressed in a cute fall frock with some adorable leather loafers. Only Becky could make loafers work. They even had pennies. I mean. *Really?!* The adorableness.

"Soon, yes," I replied with as much cheer as I could muster. "Just need to set this platinum pixie cut and I can get dressed."

She smiled, then sat on the fainting couch. I'd thrown Hank's ugly western blanket over it the day after I'd ridden Tyr on it. The cowboy motif made me gag, but even its repugnance couldn't clear that damn hockey player from my brain. I needed a transplant. Yes, a brain transplant. It was Halloween tomorrow. I suspected Dr. Frankenstein would be making house calls.

"Good. Good. I know that you and your parents aren't super close," she said as she primly folded her hands in her lap. I snorted. "It's really nice of you to make this effort for me."

I spun from my wig. "You and Hank are the only people I would do this for. I love you."

Her big blue eyes were watery. "I love you, too, Eli. Thank you."

"Hey, it's your birthday!" I plastered on a grin. "Now, shoo, so I can get this pixie cut set. I'll need time to primp so I look fabulous for our night out!"

She popped up, ran over, kissed me on the cheek, and then skipped out the door. Okay, maybe she didn't exactly skip, but it was perky. I wished I knew where to find some perk. All I could manage to dredge up was attitude and memories of Tyr holding me close. Neither of which would be of any use during this upcoming nightmare of a meal.

AN HOUR LATER, we were parked outside the Japanese restaurant that Becky loved. Knowing we were meeting my parents, I'd dressed down. Honestly, I was not trying to trigger them. They'd driven all the way from Bradford, Pennsylvania to spend the night with Becky and Hank. I knew they were freaked out by my fabulous gay self, but I wasn't a complete asshole. I could tone it down when need be. Also, I loved Becky and wanted her birthday to be all she wished it to be.

"You look like you fucked a Viking," Hank whispered as we made our way into the eatery.

I flashed him a glower. Speaking of Tyr was off-limits. Which he knew. Which was why he did it all the time. Brothers. Honestly.

"I'm fine." I sped up to get into the restaurant first. Mistake. As soon as I was indoors, my parents saw me. The looks of disgust were quickly hidden by middle-class Christian blasé, but I'd seen the slight wrinkling of my father's nose. It hurt. Still. A lot. But I buried it deep. They lit up when Hank and Becky entered behind me. Gone was the sad "what have we done to deserve this?" hangdog looks. Now, they were smiling and up on their feet, hugging, smooching, shaking hands. And there I stood. Outside all the affection. Ouch. Ouch. Ouch.

Hank slung an arm around me and began talking me

up as soon as we were seated. Mom and Dad were both wearing expressions like they'd sat on hedgehogs. As Hank bragged me up, I glanced from him to my father. Both were tall, husky men with dark hair and eyes, my father's Italian heritage evident in his strong nose and skin tone. Mom was more like Becky, also dark-haired but with a gentler side to her. Mom at least spoke to me. Dad merely grunted. I started admiring the other tables.

"…Halloween show tomorrow night. You two should come," Hank was saying. My sight flew from table, all neatly covered with red cloths and small lanterns, to my sire. "This would be a perfect time for you to see what Eli can do. He's got an amazing voice."

"He really does!" Becky chimed. "It's like listening to Judy Garland herself…only if Judy were a baritone. And the dresses are so beautiful. Eli is a marvelous seamster! I can't even sew a button on, yet he can create gowns and dresses."

"Eli always had an eye for the dramatic," Mom said, her gaze on her menu.

"We'll be leaving tomorrow morning," Dad stated, then shifted the conversation to something less unsettling. Becky gave me a look of commiseration. She and her family had some issues as well, nothing like mine, but she understood parental displeasure. Seemed her Bostonian family was not all the impressed with her choice of boyfriend, even if he were a vet. Go figure.

The meal dragged on as I picked at my dish of unagi. The eel was perfectly roasted and served on white rice with a rich soy sauce. I just wasn't all that hungry. I'd been picky all week, unable to drum up much enthusiasm for eating or even sewing. I still had some hemming to do on my Halloween dress. Which my parents would never see. Fuck. Whatever. Who cared? Not me.

"...manicure at the hotel spa tomorrow morning?" Mom was asking Becky.

"Oh, if you're going to do a manicure, let me give you the name of my new nail tech. She did these acrylics for me." I wiggled my beautiful French tips in the air. The lights from the lantern on the table made them sparkle. "No more drug store glue-on crap for me!"

Dad's gaze flew around the busy restaurant, then came back to me. The censure was easily seen, and I bit back any more manicure gushing. Hank gave me a look. I subtly shook my head. This wasn't the time or place. Becky was opening her gifts from my parents—a pretty pink sweater —and I wanted no drama. I wasn't mentally primed for it. The week had been too stressful, what with the flood and the unrequited yearning for Tyr Hemmingsen.

"...so soft. Thank you, I love it so much," Becky gushed as she rubbed her soft cheek against the cashmere sweater.

"It's really lovely," I said in the hopes that I could wedge myself into the family just as I'd been trying to do since I'd come out. Guess that scared, awkward queer kid who loved makeup and high heels never gave up hoping he'd be accepted. "I saw one online that was to die for. It was this soft peachy color cardigan with a striking black design. Totally sustainable. Oh! And it had a wide black leather belt! I totally gagged, then I saw the price and was like, 'Girl, you'd need to win forty pageants to even buy the *sleeve* of that!'"

Becky and Hank laughed. Mom gave me a wobbly smile. And Dad came unhinged.

"For the love of God, Elijah, must you wave around your painted fingernails as if you're proud of them?! And can you stop being so loud? These people do not care what you think of a damn woman's sweater. Maybe you should buy some men's clothes and see if that helps you straighten out!" Dad seethed, his voice barely a whisper, but it hit as hard as a shout.

Becky inhaled sharply. My mother stared at the lantern as if it held the secrets of the ancients. I lowered my head, tears blurring my sight.

Hank, bless his Boo-Yah heart, shot to his feet. Dad and Mom both gasped.

"He *is* proud of them, Dad. I'm proud of them, too!" I gaped at my older brother. "That's right. I'm super proud of Eli and his nails and his love of clothes and makeup. I'm also proud that he's a drag queen! Maybe *you* should work on being proud of him, too. Come on, Becky. We're going."

Becky rocketed to her penny loafers, grabbed her coat while leaving her gifts, and stormed out after my brother. Mom and Dad were shellshocked. I was, too, a little. The silence at our table was deafening. I certainly did not need Hank to speak for me, but I sure appreciated it. More than I would ever be able to express.

"So, I'm just going to go now because they're my ride." I pushed back from the table, got to my feet, and pulled my shimmery fall shawl around my shoulders. They said nothing. "I'm sorry that you couldn't be decent to me for two hours. I bet you're sorry, now, too."

I swept out with my chin so high I could barely see where I was going. The patrons and staff were all staring at me as I exited with aplomb. Hank and Becky were waiting for me with hugs that eased some of the sting. I clung to my brother for a few shaky moments, then got my shit together.

"Hey, they're not worth tears," Hank said as I dashed at my face.

"I know. I do, really, I do. I'm generally not this emotional." I blinked away a new round of tears. Hank gave me a shady look that made me snort like a hog. "Fine, okay, I'm an emotional puss, but not about them. I thought I had worked past that fucking need for them to accept me, but nope! There it is again. I'm sorry, Becky."

"Hey, don't you dare apologize. That was uncalled for behavior. I hope they slink back to Pennsylvania and think about what they've done here tonight. I'm super pissed at them!"

"I love you," I coughed, then hugged them both again. "Ah, my eyeliner must be ghastly." I wiped at my eyes. "Let's just go home. I really want a pint of cookie dough ice cream and some motherfucking Meryl."

Hank, Becky, and I left, then. I peeked back at the restaurant as we pulled away, wondering what, if anything, my parents would make of what had happened. Would they possibly relent and come to the show tomorrow night, if only to try to woo my brother and Becky back into their lives? And why, after all the years of snubs and cut, did my stupid heart skip a beat at the thought of them being in the audience? Why was I so stuck on other people making me happy of late? What did I care if my parents or Tyr showed up at the Halloween show? I'd made my way in life just fine now with only my brother, Becky, and my drag family at my side. My parents could shuffle off to fucking Buffalo—or Bradford, as the case may be—and Tyr could keep right on hiding in the stuffy old closet he was so set on staying in.

There would be other men. And other parents. Fine, there would never be other parents. I didn't need them. Or him. Especially him. Big dumb jock. The world was full of gorgeous men with cocks. Oodles of cock. It was literally everywhere. I certainly didn't need his. All I needed right now was ice cream, my four-thousandth viewing of *Mamma Mia*, and a box of Kleenex. In that order.

"Want some Abba?" Hank asked from the front. I nearly cried again. He knew me so well.

"Yes, please."

And just like that, "Dancing Queen" filled the car.

Chapter Nine

TYR

I SLAPPED THE ICE WITH MY STICK. AGAIN.

And just like in the first period, Ben ignored me and passed the puck to Dante. Who was not open. One of the Allentown Admirals picked it off and raced down the ice to get a quality shot on goal. Pissed off didn't even being to express how angry I was. I was livid. This shit had been going on for a week now. Ever since that altercation during skate, Ben had been a total asshole to me, both on the ice and off. My apology had fallen on deaf ears. After trying several times to offer my regrets and being snubbed, I gave up, and now we were here. Playing a home game against a team we should be beating easily, yet we were down by two goals.

It was all due to that kind of stupid, immature shit. When our line left the ice and the second line rolled over the boards, I threw myself down on the bench, pinning Ben between myself and Dante. Then I rounded on him.

"What the fuck was that shit?" I demanded, ripping off

my helmet and burying my face in a towel a trainer had tossed over my shoulder.

"Dante had a better angle for the pass," Ben icily replied.

"Bullshit!" I snapped after drying my face. I balled the towel up in my right hand. Ben stared out at the ice instead of looking at me. I threw Dante a questioning look. He sighed, shrugged, and shook his head. "Ben, this is going too far. I know you're mad at me but—"

"Mad?" he asked innocently, his gaze finally touching on me. His face was tight, sweaty, and free of any emotion at all. "I'm not mad. You were right to punch me in the face. Tens of thousands of dollars of dental repairs was totally justified. I mean, hey, everyone who hears a joke and doesn't laugh punches the comic, right? See it all the time."

I wanted to scream. Him playing the victim was getting old. "Ben, you said a slur."

"It wasn't a slur, it was a joke. That's what's wrong with the world. People can't even make a joke anymore without someone calling them a bigot of some sort."

"Dude, the joke was offensive," Dante spoke up, which made the muscles in Ben's neck tighten.

"I never even finished it." Ben whipped a glower my way. "You just threw a punch the minute you heard me say…" He glanced over my shoulder. Coach stood about a foot away, talking with the associate coach. "When you heard me say fag. Which I know is upsetting, especially to someone who's probably a cocksucker."

Dante slapped a hand to my chest when I went to stand up. His wide eyes were screaming at me to sit my ass down.

I glanced over my shoulder to find two coaches staring at me. I sat, my hands curled into fists, my heart thudding against my breast. Ben sneered and nodded to himself. I had to get my shit together. I'd been on a hair trigger for over a week now, and it was affecting my life and my game.

"Is there a problem down here?" Coach asked, his hands coming to rest on Ben's left and my right shoulder.

"Nope, everything is hunky dory, Coach," Ben replied with a grin. Coach looked at me. I nodded, my teeth grinding. "T and I were just discussing the impact of toxic masculinity on the sporting world."

"How about you two talk hockey and leave the PC stuff off the ice? In case you missed it, we're behind and you two are playing like my twins. They're three. Get your shit together or I'm going to break this line up."

"Yes, Coach," we both said in unison. Instead of talking to Ben anymore—what was the point—I doused my head with water, took a slug of sports drink, spit, and slammed my helmet back on. It was nearly time for us to take to the ice again. I had to regain some focus.

When the fourth line came off, we went out. Dante and I lined up a few feet from Ben, who was taking the faceoff. The ref waved Ben out. I skated up as Ben took my slot.

"You got domestic problems?" Marcus Miller, the Admirals center, asked as I bent over and placed my stick to the ice. "Rumor has it you knocked out a few of his chiclets."

"Rumors are right. He kept making stupid comments about domestic problems." I looked up. Miller smiled, his mouthguard a bright green to match his jersey. It made him look like he had moss on his teeth.

"Good on you," Miller muttered, then won the faceoff.

Which was pretty much how the whole game went; loss after loss after loss. Losing faceoffs. Losing board battles. Losing our tempers. Losing the game.

"Guess we were hexed," Dante shouted as we plodded into the dressing room.

"No treats out there tonight," someone said, which instantly brought an image of a purple and black dress to mind. Was Eli in that dress right now? Was he on stage, singing about love lost? Was he thinking of me? God knows, I couldn't get him out of my mind. I dreamt of him nightly. Hot, erotic dreams that left me hard and panting when I jerked awake with a groan night after night.

I showered and changed, the mood inside the Wilmington Bank Center low. We'd slipped to second place over the past week. A lot of that slide was squarely on Ben and me, but I had no idea how to fix things. I'd apologized several times. I'd offered to pay for all of his dental work, but our insurance would cover that, as it happened on the ice. Dante had no thoughts on the matter, either. He'd also tried to ease Ben and I into a détente but to no avail. Confused, edgy, and unable to find respite from whatever it was chewing on me, I left the arena, eager for the cold air of October on my face. I no sooner stepped outside and my phone buzzed with an incoming text.

It was Janine. I paused on my way to my car, reading over her invitation several times. She was waiting for me at her place in costume. I stared at the image that was slowly loading. A long, shapely leg in a white stocking and garter set appeared. No high heels, just a tiny foot pointed like a ballerina. Another image appeared, this one of her thigh.

J ~ I'm a naughty nurse tonight. Do you need medical attention?

I tried. Hand to the gods, I tried. I stood there in the cold, breath misting in front of me, and I stared at her leg intently. It was a shapely leg. Lovely and long. And yet it did nothing for me. No matter how I willed myself to get hard over what any other man on this team would drool over, there was nothing happening below the belt. I stewed over how to reply. She'd never been this forward before. Probably the poor woman was tired of waiting for me to make a move on her. It was unfair of me to do this to her. I should break it off now, before it got really ugly. Before she demanded to know why I wasn't turned on by her. Before the accusations started, before the tears and the pain.

Glancing up at the crystal-clear sky, I found the Big Dipper. My gaze lingered on the twinkling stars. Even with the lights of the rink and surrounding city, the constellation was plainly visible. The night skies held no answers. Drawing in a steadying breath, I typed out a short reply, erased it, typed something else, deleted that as well, and then finally sent the text that needed to be sent.

T~ We should talk about us.

I hit send, then looked to the sky once more, looking for some godly guidance. This was never easy. I'd have to drive to her place, sit her down, and give her the trite little, "It's not you, it's me. Hockey is taking all my time. It's not fair to you" speech. It was terrible. Each time I had to do it, another layer of my humanity was scrubbed away.

J~ OMG. Are you breaking up with me via text?!

I blinked at the screen.

T~ No, of course not.

J~ Fuck you. You so are. We should talk. I know what that means.

I rolled my eyes to the heavens. *A little help here, Thor? I see your cart up there. Don't leave me hanging here, buddy.*

T~ If you'd just calm down...

J~ FUCK YOU!! Don't you patronize me you fucking asshole!

Shit. Perhaps that wasn't the best thing to text.

T~ Janine if you'd let me explain in person what is going on.

Five minutes passed as the text sat there unanswered. Fingers chilly, mood sour, I stormed to my Mustang Mach-E and threw myself in. It still had that new car smell. It should. I'd just driven it off the lot yesterday. I didn't know what to do. If I drove to her place, she'd refuse to let me in, and I was not going to conduct this talk for all the world to hear. I sent her another text.

Someone pounded on my window, scaring the shit out of me. I leapt and bobbled my phone. It flew from my hands to the floor. I threw a dark look at the window to find Dante glowering at me through the steamy glass. I turned the key to AUX and pressed the window button as I bent to pick up my phone.

"Dude, honestly, is this the way you break up with a chick? I mean, seriously. You date her for months, then end it with a fucking text?!"

"I...what? How do you even know?" He cocked a dark eyebrow. Ah yes, of course. Janine and Maya had become friends. "Oh, yes, she told Maya." Dante nodded but his face was still quite angry. "In my defense, I did not break up with her with text. I told her we should talk and asked to come over to explain, but she never replied."

"Really?" Some of the ire leeched away. I handed him my phone. His eyes skimmed the conversation. "Okay, see, this is not at all what she told Maya. I knew you wouldn't be that cold to her, even if you have been a fucking miserable ass the past couple of weeks."

"I'm not miserable, I'm just…sorting things. In my life." I wanted to drive away now. This had suddenly taken a dangerous turn into highly personal Tyr matters.

"Yeah, I know. And that kind of sorting can be tough." He handed me my phone back, then bent down to rest his forearms on the door. He smelled like that seafaring cologne he always wore. The fact that he wore a nautical scent when he hated the water amused me to no end and I teased him about it all the time. "Look, I know this is none of my business. If you weren't feeling it with Janine, then for sure move on. And you did ask for a face-to-face. I will tell my girl that."

"Thank you."

He smiled, then grabbed my shoulder, squeezing it gently. "You're welcome. And for what it's worth, when you do get your life sorting done, I will still be your best friend and sidekick. No matter what you're sorting reveals. You hearing me?"

I bobbed my head. He patted my neck, then straightened up. "Good. Now go get your ass sorted. We'll never get the fuck out of Wilmington if we keep playing the way we are."

"I'm sorry if I'm holding you back from your goals," I whispered. He reached into the car to slap the back of my head. It kind of hurt.

"No one is responsible for what other people do."

"Yes, no, of course, I just…" I floundered a bit, then

simply nodded. "Yes, you're right. We'll get to the pros. I promise you, just as I promised my father."

"You just worry about the promises that you make to yourself, right? Your life won't ever be right if you're not honest about who you are. To you. Worry about Tyr. Get him settled. Stop working so hard to reach goals that might not be yours."

"I will. I'll worry about me."

"Do that. Make Tyr happy and the rest will follow. Damn, listen to me channeling En Vogue!" He laughed, then danced all the way to his car, spun around, then bowed. I had to laugh at the fool. He pulled away with a toot of his horn. I sat there for a long time, watching the other players and coaching staff leaving the barn. Soon, it was just me sitting in the dark, the only light from a streetlamp a few hundred feet away. What Dante had said kept spinning around inside my head as I cranked the engine over and left the rink, driving aimlessly around Wilmington.

Worry about Tyr.

I did worry about him. All the time. About his secret getting out. I suspected that was not what my friend had meant, though. He wanted me to worry about myself instead of others. To find what I wanted in life. But what *was* it that I wanted? Yes, to make the pros, but why? Was it what *I* wanted or was it what my father had drummed into me from the time I was old enough to hold a stick? And what about the other Tyr? The secret one that was locked in a cage in a damp, cold, lonely basement. That Tyr was a part of me. A large part. A part that was crying out for something more. Crying out to be seen, heard, recognized. Crying out to be free. Much like poor Fenrir, I felt chained. Would anyone free me? *Who* would hear me?

Eli would hear you. He's already heard your cries for companionship and gave himself to you without reserve.

Eli. Yes. Perhaps he would free me. Or at least listen. He had cared a little, it seemed. Perhaps more than a little. Just as I cared for him more than a little. Eli and the people in the Campo would hear me: they'd understand. I twisted the wheel sharply to the right after passing Rockwood Mansion. How had I gotten so far north?

I cannot even put into words the emotions that were lodged in my breast that broke free when I saw those bold, red, beautiful neon lips. I nearly ran up over the curb in my teary haste to park. Tears filled my eyes. I couldn't recall the last time that I'd wept. When my mother had died. I'd been given a small bit of time to mourn, but Uncle Jens frowned on boys who cried and so I stopped. Pawing through the glovebox of my new car, I thankfully found a courtesy package of tissues along with the paperwork. I dabbed my face, closed my eyes, and got myself calmed. Then, I stepped out into the night and into what might be a new future. I didn't know how I would be greeted here. The doorman let me right in without any hassles. Maybe Eli hadn't told the world that I'd fucked and forgotten him. Which was not true, of course. He'd been on my mind steadily, day and night, all through the night, if I were being honest. Both of us had claimed to want that one night. Maybe he still did. It would hurt badly, but if he insisted on not dating a fan, I'd back off. We could be friends.

I paused just inside the door, my ears instantly picking up Gigi's husky voice. It was incredible the effect just hearing Eli had on my body. My skin warmed, my breathing spiked, and my cock stirred. Janine's bare thigh had done nothing, but the sultry sound of Gigi talking about the final act of the Hallow-Queen Spectacular set my blood on fire. If ever I needed proof that I was gay, there it was. Not that I needed proof.

I nudged my way through the standing room only crowd so that I could get closer to the stage. When I broke through, mumbling apologies to the grunts and comments from patrons, I froze beside the bar. Gigi was indeed on stage, with other queens—Monique and Clarice plus others I wasn't familiar with yet—but she was not in her purple and black gown. A wave of disappointment crashed over me but was quickly washed away by pure lust.

She looked hot as hell in a 1940s World War 2 WAC uniform. Drag style, of course. The green jacket and skirt hugged her round hips, ass, and breasts. Her ginger hair was piled up, a small green cap sat jauntily on her head, and her lips were red as an apple. My gaze roamed over her, green cap to black open-toed heels. All I could think about was peeling that skirt and jacket off to reveal the lithe male form hidden underneath.

"You might want to dump this over your head," Cord called from the bar, reaching over to hand me a Sprite with lots of ice and a lemon wedge. I felt my face heat up but gratefully took the soda and downed half of it.

"Is it over?" I yelled over the hoots of the crowd as the girls on stage launched into a campy version of Rhianna's "Disturbia" that got the patrons up on their feet. How the hell the queens could dance like that in high heels was a mystery.

"Last song," Cord shouted back before returning to the other people calling for drinks.

I moseyed around the outskirts of the crowd, head down but eyes up, sipping my soda, my body humming with something that I'd not felt since the last time I'd seen Gigi. A guy slapped me on the back. A woman who may have been a little drunk kissed me on the cheek and tried to pull me into a three-way twerk with her and her wife. I politely skittered around them, then looked up at the stage. And right into bittersweet brown eyes. Gigi didn't miss a step, although her finely drawn eyebrows did fly upward briefly. I smiled softly as she spun, then did this crazy sort of falling down move, in sync with the other queens, that made everyone in the club hoot and clap. She laid there panting for a moment, then got to her feet. Taking the hands of her sisters, Gigi bowed deeply, threw kisses to the crowd, then rushed off the stage. The lights dimmed, a blowsy black background with the Campo Royale lips appeared on the screen.

"No one does a death drop like Gigi Patel LeBay." I nearly choked on my Sprite when Sitka's deep voice blew past my ear. I turned to look at her. She was not entirely pleased to see me, by the look on her face. She was done up as a circus ringmaster, which was fitting, I supposed. That whip in her hand was worrisome. "Are you here to see the show or Elijah?"

"Both."

Her long nose wrinkled. My gaze darted back to the whip she was clutching. "If you truly like the boy, then leave now. Dating fans is never good. Dating closeted jocks is even worse. Finish your soda and go back to the little lady who's acting as your beard. Leave my girls alone."

"I'm not dating her. That little lady. She broke up with me. I just wanted to talk to Eli, just talk." I raised a hand, palm up. "I'm in this place…mentally."

"Aren't we all," she tossed out, her dislike of me wafting off her. Which didn't seem entirely fair to me, as Eli had been fully into our one night. I'd not forced him, coerced him, or made him false promises. Nor he me. She stared right into my soul. "Ugh, fucking Christ. Repressed queers. Honestly, I should have Eladio escort you out and be done with you."

"I thought you would understand."

She rolled her lined eyes. "Please, don't play that card with me." Her lips flattened. I waited, drink in hand, for her verdict. If she said I had to go, I would. I'd not cause trouble for her or her club.

"I want to fit in here. I think…" I glanced at the logo on the screen behind the stage. "I think I could find myself here. With other people. Like me."

"And what exactly *are* you, Tyr Hemmingsen?" The word stuck in my throat. "Until you're ready to say it, keep away from my child."

She took four steps.

"Gay. I'm gay!" I barked at the back of the huge, blonde, curly wig Sitka wore. She stopped dead. I held my breath, terrified that someone had heard me, yet lighter inside than I had been in…fuck. Forever. "I'm gay. And scared. I only want to talk with Eli. He's…he's…I feel something for him, with him. If he doesn't want to see me, I'll go and never come back."

The crowd was talking away as Sitka and I had our

moment. Not a soul had looked at me after I'd blurted out my truth. She slowly turned, folded her arms over her massive breasts, then hit me with a long, level look.

"Tell Eladio that you're a nervous kitty boy. He'll let you past and you may knock on the dressing room door and request to speak to my child. If Elijah says no, you leave or you will be escorted out. If Elijah says no, you do not come back nor do you stalk, harass, or try to contact that boy. You do not want a surly drag mother on your tight ass."

"Yes, no, yes, I don't want you on my ass." A slim eyebrow rose. "Not that you're not beautiful and wise, because you are. All those things. Protective and kind."

She stuck a finger into her mouth and fake gagged. "Ugh, stop. I'm this close to drowning in the innocent sugary-sweet syrup of you. Go. See if Elijah will speak with you. I'll be watching."

"Yes, ma'am."

"Mother. You will call me Mother Sitka."

"Yes, Mother Sitka. Thank you." I tugged my beret, then ran to the corridor that led to the dressing area. The lines for the ladies' room was long, yet again. I wiggled past several people, smiling back at them, until I ran into Eladio at the dressing room door.

"Mother Sitka said I was a nervous kitty boy. I wanted to speak to Elijah," I repeated to the massive mound of bouncer. He gave me a bored look, then rapped on the door behind him, never once leaving his stool. The door cracked open to reveal a bright-eyed pudgy queen dressed like Pippi Longstocking.

"Nervous kitty boy for Gigi," Eladio grunted, his steely gaze locked on me. I pulled off my hat, holding it in front of me while Pippi went in search of Gigi. My nerves were jittery, my stomach flipping over on itself. What would I say to Eli now that I had this one chance? How could I make him understand what kind of turmoil my life and soul were in? My eyes darted from the floor to Eli when the door reopened. He was still in wig and makeup but no WAC costume. He was wearing a really ugly robe that had makeup, powder, and something that might have been toothpaste on it.

His dark eyes rounded. "How did you get back here?"

"I'm a nervous kitty boy, it seems," I replied as I drank him in. I wanted to hold him close, kiss that lipstick off his mouth, and tell him…everything. Emotions were burbling up inside me, threatening to burst free. "My heart is…" I thumped my chest. "I missed you. I don't want to just be a one-night thing with you. I'm going through…" I had to pause and inhale. "I'm not sure what I want to say other than I need you. To talk to you. I'm gay."

"I know." Eli shifted a little, sliding out of the door then closing it behind him and leaning on it. Eladio sat on his stool, watching us with complete indifference. Did he see hockey players confessing their hearts to drag queens so often that it was commonplace? "I know you're gay. And I don't want a one-night thing with you, either."

"Really?" The weight on my chest began to lessen.

"Really."

"Really?" I asked again, because life was generally not this good to me.

"He said really. Now either kiss and make up or haul your ass to the bar. You're blocking my view of the TV," Eladio huffed. I glanced to the right and, yes, there was a small TV in the corner. Was he watching a telenovela? "Don't fucking judge me, kitty boy."

What exactly was a "nervous kitty boy" and was I now part of some sort of club? My musings about if I needed whiskers was cut short when Eli climbed up over me as if I were a jungle gym. His soft, pink lips slammed over mine. I gasped and he slid his tongue into my mouth. I grabbed his ass, cradling him as we stumbled around, bouncing off Eladio, sucking on each other's tongues. Finally, I found a wall. Eli's back met it. He fisted my hair, bit my lower lip, and then licked his way back into my mouth. I leaned into him, pressing my hard cock into his. I rocked. He groaned. Eladio cleared his throat.

"You've seen worse," Eli panted over my shoulder to the doorman. Then, his gaze met mine. His eyes were warm, sweet, and welcoming. "Let's go somewhere and talk."

"My place."

He rubbed his cheek against mine. "Mm, I love that beard. Yes, your place. Give me about thirty minutes. Meet me at the bar. I missed you. I cried."

"I'm sorry," I whispered, resting my brow to his.

"Me, too. I'm sorry. Let's go to your place and talk."

I lowered his tiny feet to the floor, backed away, and then bent down to pick up my cap. Eli was smiling when I straightened.

"I lost my head over you," I tossed out with a wave of my hat.

"You lost your beret, but the sentiment is making me swoony." He gave me a gentle shove on the chest. "Go talk to Cord about sporty things."

He slid back into the dressing room, giving me a

seductive look that nearly buckled my knees. When the door shut, I stood staring at it with my hat covering my erection.

"You're blocking my show again."

"Oh, sorry." I backed out of the way, turned, and made my way to the bar. The place had emptied some after the end of the show, so I hauled myself up into a stool, placed my beret back on my head, and grinned down at my fingers. Eli had kissed me. He had missed me. He wanted more than that one night too.

I suspected the next thirty minutes would take an eternity to pass.

Chapter Ten

ELI

As soon as the changing room door blew open, I knew who had arrived.

I didn't even have to look over my shoulder or stop removing my makeup. The chitter-chatter in the room died off as if my fellow queens had just seen Beelzebub arrive, looking for a lap dance.

"Will you girls clear the room, please," Mother asked. I rose. "Everyone but you, Elijah."

"Uh-oh, looks like Mother's precious angel has a tarnished halo," Monique threw out with a pleased little snicker.

"Better a tarnished halo than that turkey you have shoved into your pantyhose," I countered, motioned to her lumpy-ass padding, and then scrubbed at my lips with a removal wipe.

"Is that why her mama called her Butterball?" Clarice added. I snorted. The other girls laughed. Monique glowered, then stormed out, her snit level high.

"Go get a drink. It's on the house." Mother Sitka growled. The room cleared quickly.

"I'm thirsty as well, Mother," I said hoping she would blow right back out and get me a vodka and cranberry. But no, of course not. She deposited her regal ass into the rolling seat beside me, her top hat jaunty and unmoving when she tipped her head. "I mean thirsty. Not *thirsty.*"

"I know what you mean, Elijah." She sighed deeply, then placed her whip across her thighs. She was still a striking queen, even though she was now in her fifties. What a life she had lived, each year of that life showed at times, like now, when she was worried about one of her drag daughters. "Are we sure about that man?"

I rolled up the wipe and tossed it into a trash can by my feet. Then I turned on my little stool and looked her in the eye.

"I think so. I've not been able to clear him from my head. I know the rules! I do." I grabbed her gloved hands and squeezed them. "And I know they're there for our safety, but Tyr is—"

"Different, yes, I know. They're all different, darling, until they're not."

I let that one go. She'd been hurt in her past, badly, by a man who'd been an admirer of her Sitka persona. That was all that I knew. Mother never went into detail and it was rude for a daughter to pry.

"He's not a fan." Her look told me how stupid she thought my comment had been. "No, he's not. Well, he is, yes. He likes Gigi and finds her attractive, but he likes me, too. Me. Elijah. And I like him too, Mother. So damn much!"

"That's obvious, pet, but…" She drew in a breath,

shook her head gently, and then exhaled. "Then you best go meet him and do what it is you youngsters do. But try to go slowly. Don't give him your heart right out of the gate. Promise me."

"I promise." It was a lie. My heart was already his, if he wanted it. Dangerous? Oh, hell yes, but I'd fallen fast and hard.

"You're such a terrible liar." She bussed my cheek so not to smear her lipstick. "If this falls apart, I reserve the right to tell you that I told you so when you show up at my door in tears."

"I'd expect nothing less from a salty old cow like you." We hugged each other. She drew back, adjusted her little top hat, and rose to her stiletto boots.

"Such an impertinent chit." She patted my cheek then left in a cloud of perfume.

I gave myself a long, assessing look in my lighted mirror. I looked happy. Would that feeling last? Getting involved with a closeted man was going to be hard. Might there be tears? Oh yes, there might be. But the way I felt when he gave me that shy smile of his wiped all my worries away. Well, not all of them, but enough that I raced to change into street clothes then darted out to the bar. There were several greedy bitches gathered around my Viking, all batting their lashes and rubbing their titties on him.

"Excuse *me*!" I snapped, elbowing a bitch or two out of the way. Tyr was beet red, his massive shoulders up near his ears, which were also scarlet. "Get. All of you whores. Get back to your street corners!" The crowd dispersed. "Why do we even allow straight women into this club? Come in here and steal our makeup tips and move on our men," I muttered as I wedged myself tight to Tyr's side. Tight to his side meaning I hung myself over him like a fucking sable coat to drive home the message to any female still harboring ideas.

"Am I really?" he asked, passing me a freshly made vodka and cranberry. He was so considerate. And hot. I wanted to explore all his nooks and crannies. With my tongue.

"Are you really what?" I stayed glued to his side to ward off a small group of single gay men passing by, giving him the eye. "Move along you fags. Go, shoo!"

"Eli, you shouldn't use that word," Tyr gasped.

"I'm allowed. I am one and I used it with love. Go on! I mean it, you little ponce!" I tossed my stirrer at the skinny twink giving Tyr the come hither. "I've reclaimed it." Tyr mumbled something into his soda glass. I went to my toes to kiss his beardy cheek. Mm, I loved whisker rub. "Does it really bother you that much?"

"It's just that…I punched someone in the face for using it not that long ago."

I climbed up into the stool next to him, keeping my eye on the blond twink, and tapped Tyr on the bicep. His head turned toward me.

"Is that what happened with your hand?" He nodded. "You told me it was a slash."

"I didn't want you to run off when you found out how violent I am."

Wow, that was brutally honest. "Well, I'm not fond of the violence of your profession." I crossed one leg over the other, catching his glance at my thighs. I did love a nice, tight legging that showcased my gams. "But you're not a violent man at heart. And I'm sure the jerk who said it meant it to hurt."

"It makes me wince when I hear it. I've never heard that term used playfully before."

I grabbed a new stirrer from Cord's little napkin/stirrer/coaster holder to chew on. "Okay, I won't use it again. I *will* use other terms such as flit, poof, Nancy boy, or shirt lifter."

"And ponce."

"Mm, yes, and ponce."

"Thanks. So, am I?"

I took a sip of my cocktail, my sight on Tyr's thick thighs. "Are you what?"

"Your man."

My gaze flew from his legs to his face. What a beautiful, masculine face it was. I'd been a dolt to listen to Sitka. Screw her and all her well-meaning rules. I wanted to date this man *hard*.

"Maybe," I replied coyly. His nostrils flared. My dick started to get fat. "Do you think you can keep up being my man? I'm really high maintenance, marginally bitchy and—"

"*Marginally?*" Cord tossed out while shooting soda into a glass.

"Fuck off." I whipped another stirrer. "Ignore the barkeep. I'm only marginally bitchy. You think you can put up with a queen like me?"

"Yes, I think so. I want to try." He was so earnest. And so scared. I could see the fear at the edges of his words and in the way he sat hunched up, cap down. This was going to take a lot of work. Perhaps I was being a romantic fool. It wasn't up to me to save this man. That he would have to do on his own. I could hold his hand as he worked his way out of the undertow and swam to shore. Oh. Swimming with one hand would make it hard, but I knew what I meant.

"Then let's go try. I think I need you to remind me just how gay you are." I popped my tongue, slid out of the bar stool, and swished my way toward the front door. I didn't need to look back. I knew he'd be coming along shortly. I was tapping away on my Uber app when he appeared beside me, opening the front door and holding it like a proper gentleman should.

"Thank you. Let me just get us a ride and—"

"I have a car. A new one. I bought it yesterday." I glanced up from my phone as a wind right off a penguin's ass blew down the street. Fuck. I needed a thicker coat. I burrowed into my shawl for warmth. "You're cold. Come on. It's just here."

"Wow, this is lush." I sank into the passenger seat after he popped the locks. He ran around the front of the car, then dove in, hurrying to crank the engine and get the heater on. "It's posh."

"Thank you. I've been trying to be environmentally conscious and use only public transportation but it's hard to try to date someone and not have a car."

"You were so sure we'd be dating?" I teased. His face fell. "I'm poking fun. And I'm more than a little flattered. This is a gorgeous car, and you bought it so you could woo me."

"Thank you. It's electric."

"The car or the wooing?" I pulled the seatbelt across my chest.

"The car."

"Pity. We'll work on your wooing." I gave him a wink that made him stammer. Shit, but he was adorable. "Let's get to your place. I'm in a hurry to see if you remember what I like."

FIFTEEN MINUTES LATER, I was sure he recalled what I liked.

We'd barely gotten up the stairs and into his place when I found myself being kissed into a frenzy as my clothing was tidily removed from my body. We hit a small snag with my leggings which required some dancing, pulling, and cursing but I finally was freed. I gave him a spin and some face, fluttering my hands over my cheeks as his gaze touched every bit of skin I had.

"Am I as beautiful as you remember?"

"More so." He yanked his shirt over his head. And that was all I could stand. I pounced on him like a cat spying a wounded mouse. He gathered me up as I licked into his mouth, his fingers biting into my ass, and carried me to his bedroom as we tongue fucked each other. Honestly, I could not tell you what color scheme his place was, or if it even had windows. I assumed it did. Who cared if it didn't? Sunlight was highly overrated and caused wrinkles.

He grunted when his knees hit the bed. I cooed. Then we were on the mattress, his hips rolling steadily, grinding that fat, long cock of his into my hip bone. I dug at his shoulders, his neck, his back. I nipped, bit, and suckled. I wanted him marked and naked.

"Get your pants off," I snarled, sucking madly on his

collarbone. We jerked and tugged at his trousers, tossing them, his belt, and his sexy gray briefs away. "Socks. No socks. I will not fuck a man with socks on." I gave him a shove, not that it moved him, but he rolled to his back.

I climbed over him, my cock leaking a trail of precum over his hip and belly. "You're so beautiful, Eli." He brushed sweaty blue hair from my face. I kissed him on the mouth, then began moving lower as he writhed under me. I flicked and nibbled on his nipples, then continued my path to my goal. His chest and belly were furry and warm. I buried my face in his stomach, the hard muscles twitching as I wiggled my hips between his thighs. "Oh, God."

His whole body twitched violently when I slithered down further. His cock was thick, hard, and right there in my face. I gobbled him down ravenously. His hand came to rest on my head, fitting over my skull like a cap, yet he didn't shove or push me down. He didn't need to. I had a well-trained gag reflex. He moaned when I took all of him down my throat.

I cupped his balls as I sucked away madly, tugging on the heavy orbs, until he was speaking in Danish. Then I pulled off his dick and feasted on his balls. I pressed his cock to his belly, took one ball then the other into my mouth. He cried out a warning. I assumed it was about him being close. It was all Dane, so I wasn't sure, but the pulsing of his cock was signal enough. I grabbed his dick and stroked it, closing my eyes as he coated my face with thick ropes of spunk.

"Oh, fuck!" He roared. I knew that word. He bucked me off, scooped me up, and tossed me to the bed, moving over me like a hungry lion. I purred like a cat full of cream, then I licked a dollop of cum off my lower lip. Tyr laved my face, licking off his spunk, and then slipped me his tongue.

"Delicious," I whispered when we broke apart.

"Do that to me. Come on my face. Please." He flipped us over, taking my hips in his hands he nudged me upward. I sat on his wide chest then fed him my dick. He was so greedy for it, he gagged a few times before he found his depth. I began thrusting, my orgasm just a few moments away. He wanted more and moved me up and off his chest. Knees resting by his ears, hands on the wall behind his bed, I gave him more cock. His eyes were closed now, his lips stretched around my prick. I dug at the walls, my acrylic nails raking over the wallpaper.

"Oh, shit…shit," I cried out when my balls drew up. I sat back, wet dick sliding from between his lips, and grabbed my cock. Tyr opened his eyes, smiled, and let his mouth drift open wider. "Shit!" I yelped as I pumped. Cum speckled his cheeks, beard, nose, eyelashes, and lips. I gave him just the head. He suckled hard like a babe taking a bottle. I jerked and shuddered, my balls emptying into his warm mouth. "So good…so good…so good."

"Mmmm," he hummed around my dick, pulling another spurt from my already flagging cock. I fell forward, rasping, spent, my forehead on the headboard. Huh, he had a headboard. Nice one, too. Wooden. Christ. That was fucking incredible. I shimmied down a bit, until I could plaster my mouth over his. Our tastes merged. It was glorious. Delicious. Succulent. He moved us around, placing me where he wished on the bed with incredible ease. I loved it so much, I just melted into him, my lips moving over his neck and face as he tenderly lifted me from the bed and carried me to the bathroom.

"Are we going to play in the shower?" I throatily asked, my lips resting on his throat.

"Maybe." We slid into the small bath sideways, my feet only touching the floor once we were in the room fully. He kissed me softly, searching deep inside my mouth. "I love the taste of you, of me on your tongue. I think I'm addicted to you."

"Same, oh, the same!" I wound my fingers in his hair to smash his mouth back to mine. How we ever managed to get into the shower without falling and breaking our necks, I couldn't say. A light came on, he kissed me. The water came on behind me. He kissed me. The plaid curtain —who the hell had a plaid shower curtain in a soft pink bathroom, oh, god, spare my poor eyes now—slid over the rod. He kissed me. I stepped in. He stepped in. And then he kissed me. I was beginning to sound like that song by The Crystals circa 1963 or thereabouts.

"Let me wash my face," he said, then tenderly peeled me off him. All kinds of randy thoughts entered my head but nothing naughty took place. He took the bar of green soap, lathered his hands, and scrubbed his face, raking at this beard with his nails after handing the soap to me. I began soaping his chest; the fur on his pectorals bubbled nicely. He stood still, arms up over his head, soap clinging to his eyelashes, smiling as if he had fallen into a vat of pure sweet creamy butter. Mm, I loved butter. Thinking of it made my stomach rumble.

"You're hungry," he stated as I washed his abs.

"A little. I skipped lunch." He found my hands on his belly, gently took the soap, and then began quickly washing his legs and feet. I stood back, arms folded, feeling a little put out. "I can do that. I wanted to get you all soapy then drop to my knees to suck your balls until you came."

He stopped washing to look at me. "You need to eat." And he went back to rubbing the bar of soap over his thighs. Mm, they were such nice legs. All muscular and covered with dark brown hair. Just like his balls. Yummy. My tummy growled again. "See."

"Fine, but once you feed me, I want more of this." I cupped his soapy nuts and cock. He grunted, a wicked smile playing on his lips.

"I can do that." He kissed my face, his aim a little off as his lips found my eye. I snorted in amusement and the shower became more about washing and rinsing and less about round two. He stepped out to let me rinse off, then handed me a towel when the water was off. "Let me find you something to wear."

"Oh! Let me pick it!" I bounced around the bath, darting under his arm, to race to his bedroom which was tidy as a pin. Oh, dear. And me being such a slob. That might cause tension when we live together.

Hit the brakes, you daffy dame! Live together? Dear God, this is your second hookup. Don't be picking out drapes yet.

Fuck off cow bag. This isn't a hookup, it's a...well, I'm not sure yet. Oh! A reconciliation! Yes. It's a reconciliation and you're really dampening my mood.

"I like your bedroom," I tossed out, skipping to his closet, naked as a newborn penguin. Did they have hair or feathers? Whatever. My ass was bare. "It's very blue."

"Yeah, Maya helped decorate it." He padded in behind me, a thick towel around his lean waist.

I thew the closet door open, then gave him a look over my damp shoulder. "Who is this Maya? Do I have to cut a bitch? I will. I have the sharpest eyebrow pencil this side of the Pecos. Oh! This. I want to wear this!"

I pulled a hockey jersey off a hanger. It was red, white and had DANMARK under a regal looking lion on the front. His last name on the back over a huge 18. I pulled it on, then sniggered at the fit. The sleeves hid my hands, the shoulder seams were nearly to my elbows, and the hem of the jersey was at my knees. It was perfect!

"Ah, that's special. I wore that at the Olympics three years ago." He reached out to run his finger along my lower lip. I playfully nipped at it. He smiled, then slid an arm around my middle.

"Did your team win?" He swept me up off my feet. "Shit! Tyr, I can walk."

"But you'd rather be carried, I suspect."

"You have me there. If it were possible, I'd be transported from pageant to pageant in a palanquin with two massive men in tiny loincloths toting me hither and yon!"

"See, I knew it. I'm getting you figured out."

We walked through a rather blasé living room. Tan and white and brown. This Maya was boring. Speaking of which…

"So, Maya?"

"Is my friend Dante's girlfriend since forever."

"Okay. She's allowed to decorate your place, but she is lacking in panache. You should let me decorate."

He placed me on a throw rug in front of a silver stove. I gawked at the kitchen. Nice, clean, sparkly clean even, but again, lacking any personality.

"Do you like eggs?"

"Yes, eggs are yummy. Can you scramble them and melt cheese on them? Thank you. Love you." I moved around the room, touching this and that, as he pulled out a frying pan then rummaged around inside a big silver fridge. "This is a nice place. How long have you been here?" I opened a drawer. All the silverware was in a tray, all tidy.

"A while, now."

"It's roomy," I called out as I meandered into the tan living room. "Must cost a pretty penny. Do you make millions?" I studied some old photos in a wall collage above the sofa. A young boy, his parents, all smiling. A perfectly posed image by a frosty lake. The older man and boy were in hockey gear. The woman in knitted hat and mittens. Tyr looked just like his father, right down to the set of his lips on his face.

"Millions? No." He laughed, the happy sound bouncing off the white walls. I poked around at the books stacked neatly on shelves. Fantasy, sci-fi, and collections of fairy tales. Each shelf neatly arranged by genre. Thick bound books by Hans Christian Andersen, Brothers Grimm, as well as authors I had never heard of—Charles Perrault, Marie-Catherine d'Aulnoy, Joseph Jacobs. Then, there were notebooks stacked with the hardcovers. These were all handwritten and packed front to back with pages of tidy longhand verse. I flipped through one, eyes growing wide as I read over the fables that a young Tyr Hemmingsen had penned.

"Wow," I whispered at the imaginative prose of a young adult. His writing was straight, firm, and easy to read. And in English. Did Danish children learn a second language in school? That was impressive. I was born in the States and could barely speak my native tongue properly, let alone write in it. I gave Mr. Morton, my tenth grade English teacher, a peptic stomach. Or so he said. Probably it was Mrs. Morton, but sweet little Elijah with the pink fingernails got the blame. I bet if I could have written a story about an enchanted moth and a prince like young Tyr had, Mr. Morton might not have needed all those Rolaids.

"The eggs are ready."

I spun to face him, a battered yellow notebook in my hands. His eyes narrowed. "Sorry. I'm so sorry."

"What are you doing with that?" He crossed his arms over his chest. God, he looked fucking sexy standing there in a towel, a fire in his eyes.

"I was snooping. It's a terrible habit, I know. I do it all the time. I was just curious. I know so little about you and…" The stern look on his face didn't soften. *Shit.* "I wanted to see what kind of books you read. Then, I found the notebooks and just took a peek. Honestly, I only read a few. From when you were younger. They're incredibly good. So good! Please don't hate me. I promise I'll never snoop ever again. Not even a fast look inside your medicine cabinet when I go piddle in the night."

"Hate you? How could I possibly hate you, Eli?"

"Oh, it's easy. Ask Monique. Or my father. Crap. Don't ask him. We don't talk about him." I held out the notebook. "I'm sorry."

"It's okay. I'm just…not used to people being here." He padded over to me, his cross look fading as he lifted the old notebook from my hands. "I had to hide these for so long…"

"From whom?"

"My father." He carried the notebook to his bland tan sofa. I followed, dropping down to sit on my bent leg after he lowered himself to the couch. "He always had one goal for me; to win the Stanley Cup. Anything else, any hobbies or likes that did not have to do with hockey, were extraneous. I was allowed to read about the Norse gods, as that pleased him. He enjoyed the mythos, for it gave me tales of heroes to emulate on the ice."

"Wow, your father has severe control issues. Kind of like mine."

"Had. He died when I was thirteen. My mother a year later by her own hand."

I gasped, then covered my mouth with my hand. He glanced at me with a wistful expression. "It's tragic, I know. Everyone told me how tragic it all was."

"It really is." I took a chance. Sliding myself closer and then into his lap when he opened his arms. I nuzzled my nose under his chin, snuggling up tight, holding him close. "I'm sorry you had to hide your fables. The one I read was amazing."

"Thank you. I don't write anymore."

I kissed the side of his neck then sat up to search his face. "Why not? He's dead. He can't control what you do now."

"He will always control what I do. I made a vow." He looked so incredibly sad.

"If it's a vow that is crippling and toxic to your soul, you can break it."

"No, I can't. I've already let him down in so many ways. This vow, to win the Cup, this is something that I can do. I *must* do."

"But at what cost?" I asked. He never replied. I cupped his handsome face and led his lips to mine. The kiss was supposed to be a soft, tender peck to let him know I understood about disappointing your father. As soon as his lips touched mine, the spark leapt into a flame. Shit, this man did things to me. Marvelous, mouthwateringly magnificent things.

We never got to our cheesy scrambled eggs until well after three in the morning. Tyr took me back to bed. We made slow, slick love. I welcomed him into me with clawing need, his cock stroking in and out of my body, each thrust hitting my prostate until I burst into a hundred thousand points of light. His release followed, his big shoulders trembling, his neck bulging, his prick kicking inside me.

We cuddled a bit, warmed our eggs in the microwave, and ate them in his bed, forking fluffy bites into each other's mouths between kisses. I fell asleep wrapped in his arms and his huge DANMARK jersey and dreamed of moths, dragons, and princes that looked a great deal like my war god.

Chapter Eleven

TYR

NOVEMBER WAS ONE OF THE MOST PECULIAR MONTHS IN MY life.

Nothing was as it had been. Change was creeping into my life in small—and massive—ways, and most of it was due to a tiny firecracker of a drag queen.

Eli's presence in my life, hidden still, which was becoming more and more uncomfortable, was subtly altering how I lived. Perhaps it was taking me from a place where I merely existed and was shifting me into actually living. There were small tells, like a lipstick in my bathroom, the slow but steady disappearance of my hockey jerseys, and the smell of his rose water perfume on my sheets. Then, there were bigger signs of the shifts in my life. Now when I woke up, I wasn't keen to head to the rink, or not as keen. Hockey had been my savior for years, the one and only way I found any kind of redemption, the only way I could possibly stop being a failure. Now it was a job. A job with coworkers that were sneaky and sly in their dislike of me. It upset and worried me that I was not finding the joy in the game that I had previously. It seemed I was much more concerned with Eli, the Campo Royale, and my notebooks of silly fairy tales.

But were they really silly? Or was that just my father forcing his ideals into my head? Eli seemed to think so and scolded me whenever I said that jotting down a fable was a waste of time.

"If it brings you joy, then it's not a waste of time, it's balm for the soul," he liked to say as he applied his false eyelashes or glued his eyebrows or sewed a pretty dress.

It was obvious he found great joy in drag. I admired him, yet felt a bit of envy, as well. I wanted to love my sport again, to feel the burning drive to succeed. To see my family name on the Cup. But was that what Tyr Hemmingsen truly wanted, or was that the dream Elias Hemmingsen force fed his son when he failed to attain the glory he sought? My head was full of confusion and contradictions. And change. Lots of change. Most of it for the good, I hoped.

Perhaps the biggest improvement was the fact that I now had a family of sorts. It was a small clan compromised of drag queens, barkeeps, Eli, his brother Hank, and his girlfriend Becky. Slowly but surely, like water working on wearing down a rock, this new family of my choosing was usurping my teammates. That wasn't good. Or was it? Ugh, the mayhem of my mind.

Yet, despite the upheaval, I had no wish to go back to how it was. Only a few people knew about Eli and me being a couple. Hank and Becky who had been so incredibly warm and welcoming to me, I nearly wept the first time we had a meal together. Such a stupid thing to get sentimental over. A meal, and not even a great one. A pizza and some salad followed by two hours of Monopoly. Hank and his girl never once asked more than we were willing to give. They knew we were lovers and vowed to keep my sexuality a secret until I was ready to do whatever it was I was going to do. That was the million-dollar question. What *was* I going to do?

Right now, I was enjoying a slice of pumpkin pie and coffee. Eli was on my right, Becky on my left, and Hank seated across from me at the small kitchen table. Eli's house was filled with the smells of a spectacular Thanksgiving feast. We'd stuffed ourselves to the breaking point on turkey, mashed potatoes, yams, corn, buns, and now pie. Becky was telling a story about her parents—who they were going to visit over the long weekend—that had me sniggering into my coffee.

"…fell right into the water! My mother was furious that he'd tumbled off the boat into the water. Dad and George thought it was hilarious, but my mom feared they'd never get invited back to Walker's Point after that debacle."

"And this is what I'm trying to finagle my way into. A family who vacations in Kennebunkport with ex-presidents," Hank said with a roll of his eyes.

"It's all show," Becky stated as she nibbled on some pie crust. I nodded in understanding. We all put on fronts. No one was putting on a false face bigger than mine, not even Eli, who had a whole different persona. "They'll come around, trust me. If not, they can stay home when we get married."

My eyes darted from Eli, who was licking whipped cream from his finger, to Hank. "Have you proposed?"

"No, not yet. We've talked about it, though."

He and Becky exchanged looks of love that made my full belly cramp with envy. What must it be like to be able to discuss weddings with the person you loved? Would I ever know?

Not if you stay in the closet.

"I demand to be the best man slash maid of honor," Eli chipped in, then pushed his pie away. "I cannot eat any more. I won't fit into my red gown for the Greater Manhattan Drag Association Mid-Winter pageant next week."

He'd barely eaten as it was, but there was no point to arguing. He had corsets to fit into, he would reply. It seemed silly to me that a man as lean as Eli would cinch his waist in even more, but there was a standard to maintain. Or so I had been told. Proportions, darling.

I ate his slice, moaned, and then rose to help clean up. Hank and Becky pulled out a few hours later, leaving the house to Eli and me.

"Come with me," he purred as soon as his brother was out of sight. I groaned. "It was the second slice of pie." He tugged on my arm to no avail. I had found the couch. A nap was in my future.

"I'm too full to move."

He dropped my hand with a huff. "Fine, lay out here like a sack of boiled turnips. I guess you won't get to see me model that black and purple gown you keep whining about."

That got my attention. Not enough to make me sit up, though. I really had eaten too much, but the food had been so good and the familial feelings so overwhelming that I hadn't been able to stop myself. I'd work it off tomorrow in the gym. We had a noon game that Eli was going to attend. It was insane how excited I was for him to be in the crowd. He'd be wearing my Olympic jersey, the one he slept in, the same one he was wearing now. Nothing made me giddier than seeing him in my sweaters.

"I'll nap for an hour then come see you." I teased a bit, knowing that it took him what seemed like forever to get into full drag.

"Honey, really, I am not painting a mug tonight. Have you seen my skin?!"

"It's one pimple," I replied around a yawn.

"On my nose! Just call me Hagatha the witch. No, no makeup, only the gown, corset, and stockings." Mm, stockings.

"With a garter belt?" I reached up to push my festive green beret off my face. He nodded. My dick grew hard instantly. I slowly rose from the couch. He pranced around in circles, took my wrist, and led me to his bedroom.

"Sit down on the bed. Don't touch your dick." He kissed me on the cheek, then darted to his sewing room. Making my way to the bed required stepping over high heels, a romance novel, several empty water bottles, and a jar of olives. Eli loved them. Ate them like candy. I couldn't stomach olives, so I discreetly rolled the jar under his bed in the hopes that he'd forget them like he had everything else under his bed. Kissing him after an olive binge was not pleasant.

I sat on the edge of the mattress, trying my best to ignore the debris scattered about. Messiness was not a Hemmingsen trait. My mother had been meticulous about her home, probably because cleaning gave her a sense of control that she desperately needed. Amazing what you learn as you mature. If only I'd known why she was acting as she had been back when I was a child, perhaps I could have helped in some way. Instead of tidying up Eli's creative chaos—his words not mine—I removed my cap. Then I lifted the purple boa that had been draped over the headboard, placed my beret on the post where the boa had been, and wrapped the feathery thing around my neck. My eyes closed as I inhaled the scent of rose rising from the boa. That aroma eased me. I let my breathing level out. That nap idea was returning as my body relaxed and softened. Amazing, the effect his perfume had on me…

"Those are real ostrich feathers. Sitka gave it to me as a gift, since I can only afford chicken feathers."

My eyes popped open and there he stood. The Halloween gown that I'd never seen on him hugging his curves like a second skin. He'd padded the bodice, but the waist flared outward, so it was hard to tell if he'd used hip pads. My cock stiffened as he sashayed to me, each step slow and precise.

"Do you see how I'm moving?"

"Yes." I wet my parched lips.

"Notice how I'm wearing the garment. It's not wearing me."

"Okay." All I wanted to do was drop to my knees and see what was under that voluminous skirt. And so, I did. I slipped from the bed then reached for him. He gasped and giggled as I led him to me, my hands on his slim hips. Then, I flipped the heavy skirt up over my head.

"What are you doing down there?" he asked playfully. I drew in the smell of rose, then buried my face into his groin, my chin rubbing across his dick. I heard his sharp inhalation. Reaching around, I cradled his tiny cheeks in my hands. I kissed each garter belt, each stocking, and each silken covered toe. His cock was fat now, pressing against the compression underwear he'd pulled on. The deep plum-colored panties were straining to contain his erection. So, I helped them out. I tugged the band down until his cock popped out. "Oh, holy shit, Tyr!" He yelped when I took his prick into my mouth.

I swallowed him down as far as I could, my fingers now deep in the crack of his ass, kneading his buttocks as he began to pump his hips. It had been several days for us. The team had been south for a week and had just come back home yesterday. He'd been at a pageant in Jersey until late last night, so we'd just reunited today. He'd be primed, just as I was. I unzipped my jeans, fished my dick out, and began jerking. Eli grabbed my head as well as several yards of material and began fucking my mouth with vigor. I took it all. Every inch of him. Eyes watering, spittle dripping from my chin to my cock, I worked the saliva around the head of my dick. My deep throating skills were lacking in comparison to Eli's, but he seemed to be enjoying my efforts. A hot splash of cum coated my tongue. I swallowed, sucked harder, and worked my cock with vigor. A flash of fire touched off in my balls. I arched into my fist, coating my hand.

"Oh...ah...oh, yes," Eli whimpered as he rocked in and out of my mouth, smearing spunk over my lips and chin. "Oh, hell...you *do* like this gown!"

"I like what's under it more," I replied, sliding my lips up and down the sides of his prick. "I think I might have come on your foot." It was dark under here, so I wasn't sure but...

"You did. Someone will have to remove my soiled

stocking for me. I'm so weak from all that sexual pleasure."

I chuckled softly, then cleaned his cock up the best I could before he lifted the skirt over my head. I kissed my way up to his mouth, peppering his creamy exposed shoulders with kisses before taking his face in my hands and sliding my tongue into his mouth. He mewled in pleasure then fell into my arms with a swoony sort of sigh. I picked him up.

"Such a drama queen," I teased as I carried him to bed then laid him on the rumpled coverings. He never made his bed, it seemed.

"That I am, as well as a pageant queen. Did you see the little crown I won in Jersey?" He lifted his leg for me, and yes, his stocking was wet with cum. I pushed his skirt to his upper thighs, then gently unfastened the garter belt and rolled down the stocking.

"I was under your skirt, if you remember. It's dark in there." I tossed his stocking over the headboard, then removed the other, before I kissed a path up the inside of his leg. He gasped and giggled when I nibbled at his prominent hip bone. It worried me how little he ate. He claimed to be perfectly fit, but still he consumed so few calories. Maybe I was just used to dining with hockey players...

"Dark but delightful," he sighed, then rolled to his belly. "Unzip me, will you? I'm simply too spent to move."

"Mm, too spoiled, I would say." He laughed like the imp he was. I slowly undressed him, peeling away layers of padding and a corset until I had him bared. I shucked my clothes off with haste, giving them a toss to a chair in the corner that held boots, shoes, a silver wig, two faux fur stoles, and a giant inflatable orange. When I lay down beside him, he shimmied around, plastering his small frame into my side to he could stroke the hair on my chest.

"Can you cover us? I'm growing chilled," he whispered, then pinched my right nipple. I twitched but reached down and yanked the thick duvet up. Soon, I'd be sweltering, and he'd be cold. Then, he'd pull on a jersey of mine and thick fluffy socks that didn't match the sweater. "Oh, yum. You're a true prince." His head came to rest on my chest, his fingers skipping up and down my abs. My eyes drifted shut. Rose water filled my senses. I was so happy right now. If only I could stay in bed with Eli forever. "Will you ever write a fairy tale for us?"

My eyes flew open. "I don't write anymore."

"You should. Your tales were so good! And I would love to be the star of one. Can you make one up for me?"

"Eli…"

"Please?" He kissed my chest, my neck, my chin, and then my stern lips. "Just a short one?" The man had me so firmly wrapped around his pinkie finger, it was sad. Even so, I huffed, grunted, and nodded. Eli squealed in glee and sat up, the covers sliding off his back as he rushed to find a Warthogs sweater with my name on the back. "Where are my polka dot socks?!"

"Over by the window. In the mouth of that obscene stuffed alligator."

"Oh, right!" He bounced over, grabbed the socks out of the alligator's mouth, then hurried to pull them on. Where the alligator with the dildo strapped to his middle had come from was a mystery. I'd not asked. I wasn't sure I really wanted to know. "Okay, here I am." He leaped onto the bed, spread himself out on his belly, and placed his chin in his hands. "Tell me a story. I need to be a prince. *The* prince. Obviously."

I rolled my head away from his bewitching face to study the ceiling. "Once upon a time…I feel silly."

"Please don't. Don't be ashamed of your gift. No offense but your father was wrong to stifle your creativity. Now go on, please."

"Once upon a time, there was a cross dressing prince." I still felt stupid, but if I closed my eyes, I could see a castle appearing in my mind's eye. "He was the most joyous prince in all the realms."

"And the best dressed."

"Obviously."

"And had the best mug."

"Of course. No one in the kingdom could paint a mug like Prince Elijah Gigi."

"I like that. My thighs are getting cold. Can you cover me?" I gave him a withering look. He blew a shank of blue hair from his nose. "I *am* the prince."

"So spoiled." I moved to my side, tugged the covers up over his royal ass, then lay there looking at him. He was smiling, his eyes twinkling. I loved everything about his face. "So, one day, Prince Elijah went for a ride on his royal steed."

"What kind of horse is my steed?"

I paused to think. "A unicorn that farts rainbow glitter."

"Perfect." He sighed. "I shall name him Twirly Ponyweather and he shall be the envy of all in my kingdom."

"I'm sure he is." I chucked at his enthusiasm. "So, one day the handsome prince and Twirly Ponyweather left the royal stables and set out on a ride."

"What was I wearing?" I rolled my eyes. "No, don't make fun. As the prince, my riding ensemble would be quite important. I think I would be in a flowing gown. Something very Victorian. Let me get my phone so I can do a riding habit search."

"Is what you're wearing that important?" He shot me a look. "Sorry, yes, of course it is." I waited while he searched the internet, a smile working at the corners of my mouth as he sat crossed legged and scoured the web. When he had finally decided on a riding habit that was made of red velvet with a bustle and matching red velvet top hat, we continued with his story.

The tale took on a life of its own, with magical creatures that the prince encountered along his ride through the kingdom. Eli wiggled back under the covers, rested his head on his pillow, and held my gaze throughout the telling. When I got close to the end, and the prince had kissed a cassowary who'd been hexed by an evil warlock—his choice of creatures to kiss, obviously—I could see everything so clearly in my head. The prince, his unicorn, the cassowary, the kingdom. Everything. It was rough. Extremely rough. And had no moral yet, but it could be shined up. I *desperately* wanted to write it all down.

"You look so blissful right now," he whispered as sleep began to tap him on his shoulder. "Like, the only time I see you so happy is when you look at me. You should write that down, my story, and find an artist. I know one. Clarice's boyfriend's sister's boy is incredibly good. I bet he would do the illustrations. Oh, girl! Gay fables. What every queer child needs!"

"That was just for you. I could never write a book."

"Never say never. You can do whatever *you* want, Tyr." He yawned like a sleepy kitten. "You need to break those chains that keep you unhappy. Be like that Fenris puppo you told me about."

"Fenrir was a wolf. Also, if he breaks free, it signals the beginning of Ragnarök."

"Which is what? A dish made of eels?"

"The end of the world."

"Oh. Okay, so that puppo needs to stay chained, but you don't."

His long lashes fluttered down to rest on his cheeks. I moved closer to him, my hand coming to rest on his hip as he moved into a soft, deep sleep. Watching sleep smooth his features, I lay there pondering if what he said was actually true. Could I do what *I* wanted? Openly? Imagine such a thing. Once he was sound asleep, I kissed his pink lips and went in search of a paper and pencil. Jotting down notes wasn't writing. It was just…jotting.

Chapter Twelve

ELI

I WAS OUTNUMBERED AND SURROUNDED BY ATHLETIC supporters.

Thankfully, the jersey I was wearing—the bright red and white DANMARK one—seemed to counterbalance the fact that I had eyeliner and a manicure the shady bitch behind me wished she had. In all truth, she wished she had my hand with makeup, as well, because she was not blended well *at all.* Contouring, henny. Look it up.

I was right down by the ice. My feet were chilly, but Tyr had told me to wear boots, so I'd pulled on a darling pair of pink mukluks. He'd also told me to wear a coat and bring a blanket. Also, and this he had added on as delicately at he dared, he asked me to not go overboard on my look. He was so tactful all the time. Such a refined and tender man who—

"Ack!" I screamed when two monstrous males in jerseys slammed into the glass right in front of me. The plexiglass shook madly. I was sure they were going to come breaking through and land in my lap. I threw my hands up over my face until the man beside me, an older gent in a Warthogs jersey, tapped my arm.

"It's safe. They're down at the other end of the ice," he said. I peeked through my cold fingers at him then at the still vibrating glass. "You're missing all the action down by the net."

He jerked his whiskery silver chin. I lowered my hands, looked around a big man sitting on the other side of the glass all dressed up to play hockey, but instead of wearing a helmet, he had a ballcap on. Yes, okay. The men were all down there jabbing at the man in the net with their sticks.

"This is my first live game," I told the man beside me.

"I would have never guessed." He chortled, then offered me his hand. "Morty. I'm a season ticket holder. What brings a…uhm…well, a man of your delicate sensibilities to a hockey game?"

The fans all cheered. I looked down the ice to see two men skating around in circles, fists up. Oh no. No. No. Not a fight. Oh God. I covered my face again. Please let there not be blood. I did not handle blood well. The crowd got louder and louder. How could people cheer for this? Was this what ancient Rome was like? All we needed were some lions and Russell Crowe shouting about Sparta while kicking a Persian into a pit. Or was that a different bloody warrior movie? Who cared? They all made me queasy.

"Is it over?" I asked from inside my hands when the cheers died down.

"Yep, they're both going to sit for a bit in the sin bin. So, what brings you to the game today?"

I dropped my hands to my lap. I was not going to survive this game. Would it be sissified of me to faint if someone—like Tyr—were to get sticked up the face. In the face. A stick in his rugged, handsome face. What. Ever.

"I won the ticket. On the radio. They had a contest." It was a dumb lie, but if it got us away from the *big secret*, then I'd roll with it. "They were asking for the names of three Barbra Streisand movies. Which, duh, what a simple question. *Hello Dolly*, *Funny Girl*, and *The Way We Were*." I ticked the replies off on my fingers. "Gods above, when Katie and Hubbell broke up, I was a motherfucking wreck. Tears for days."

Morty stared openly at me. Oops. Was I being too gay? I knew I should have skipped the colored lip balm, but my lips had been kissed dry before we left my house.

"You remind me of my late wife Doris."

"Oh? Did she wear pink mukluks and a knitted bunny hat to hockey games?" I truly did love my bunny hat. Tyr had given it one glance before an odd, strained stroke look overtook him. Still, he'd not asked me to not wear it. What did it matter how I dressed? No one was allowed to know we were dating. Which sucked, because I wanted to be at his side. Also, the hennies behind me kept talking about him as if he were a slab of beef. Which, yes, he was meaty and juicy like a fine prime rib, but bitches were talking about *my* boyfriend.

"No, but she did love Barbra."

We struck up an instant friendship. Morty knew his Barbra. He tried to explain the game to me as it went, but at the end, I knew little aside from the fact that hockey players were big, sexy beasts and that a puck is made out of vulcanized rubber. I would never use that information, but Morty seemed thrilled to have passed it on. I did get to see Tyr doing what he did. I wavered between being oddly turned on by him being all macho and sweaty and cringing at how physical he was. Sure, I knew it was a contact sport, but did it have to be *that* much contact?! Surely, they could poke the puck around the ice and not knock each other into next week. But who was I to say? I cheered when Morty did, booed when Morty did, and drooled whenever I got an eyeful of Tyr being war godly. The Warthogs lost in overtime. Morty was upset. I was just happy to not have had to witness Tyr getting a skate in the neck. It had happened. Google it. Hockey was a violent game.

Wandering outside after the game alone felt crummy. I wanted to go see Tyr in the locker room and ask him why he'd not played in the third period much. Morty had said he'd made a dreadful turnover. I'd nodded but didn't know what that meant. I'd personally never met a dreadful turnover. Most of them were simply delightful. All filled with warm, yummy fruit. My stomach snarled, so I hurried home to have an early dinner.

Tyr texted me as I rode the bus home to tell me he would meet me later at the club, so I stripped off my winter gear, pulled on my fluffy socks, and whipped up a fruit smoothie. I dared not gain a pound. We were coming into prime pageant season with scores of holiday shows added into the mix. All my dresses were form-fitted. There was no room for a pound anywhere. Each show and pageant was important. I needed the winnings and the notoriety. Most of my cash went right back into my drag, what I didn't need to pay my few bills, that was.

Hank carried the lion's share of the cost here. He paid the mortgage and the utilities. I paid for my phone bill. That was it. It was slightly embarrassing to be relying on my brother, but I was working my ass off just to survive. There weren't many queens who were rolling in the cash that I knew. Most worked two jobs: a day job, then the clubs at night for honing their craft. I was lucky in that I was popular here in Wilmington. The fans wanted me on the stage as often as possible, so I got a heavy rotation.

That was another bitch that Monique tossed in my face all the time. It wasn't my fault the salty bitch couldn't dance or sing. Sitka was her drag mother, as well, but she always accused me of being Mother's favorite. Maybe I was. Maybe Monique needed some sewing lessons. The ones that I had taken had just about broken my bank—the piggy one in my bedroom—but they had paid off big in pageant winnings. You can't go on stage with saggy seams or a gaping crotch. It took money to make money, as the money people say. Still, I could use more. A car would be nice.

I sighed as I cut banana slices. The lack of funds was depressing, at times. I so wanted a car, but there was no cash for one, let alone the added expense of insurance. Someday. When my star rose above the small-town clubs, I'd have one. Something shiny and sleek. Something that screamed "Gigi is here bitches!" to the world.

After my smoothie break, I packed up my gear—extra makeup, pads, costume, and shoes—and slid into Hank's truck. They'd taken Becky's Beemer to the meet the folks. The cab was freezing. While I waited for the windshield to thaw, I sent Hank a text and a picture that I had snapped with me and the ballcap wearing hockey player—Morty had explained that he was a backup goalie—with a cheery note.

E~ Wish you were here.

I tittered after sending, knowing he was going to birth a buffalo when he saw me at the game. Poor fool, stuck up there with the rich folk trying to pretend he was something he wasn't. My sniggering slowly died as a modicum of warm air began to leak out of the vents. Actually, there was nothing funny about not being able to be who you were. Seeing Tyr's struggles on a daily basis was painful, and while Hank's efforts to impress those of a higher social standing wasn't the same as hiding your core self in the dark, it certainly was similar. Why the shit couldn't people just accept others as equal? Why did the world have to be so fucking mired in class, race, and sexual segregation? I felt bad now, so I sent my brother a follow-up message.

E~ Don't let the man get you down. Will score us tix to the next game at home. XXOO

I felt marginally better and eased out of our narrow drive. On the way to the club, I rehearsed a new song that I'd added to my set. I was up first tonight. We worked on a staggered schedule so no one girl got star billing, which was generally being last. Not that I was anywhere near what some would call a warm-up act. Still, it seemed fair and saved Sitka from listening to crusty old cows ragging about lineups.

Singing along to "Get Happy" by the amazing Judy Garland—*God, do not let me screw up a Judy song; every gay in a hundred-mile radius will chase me through Delaware with flaming torches*—I was feeling a little uneasy as I jockeyed the monster Ford pickup into a parking slot in the employees parking area behind the Campo.

"You're just too big and that's not something that one generally hears coming from me," I told the truck as I gathered my paraphernalia and raced into the back door. I'd just rounded a corner when I bumped into Sitka studying the fuse box panel. Her gaze met mine. She was not ready for her MC duties. My eyes rounded to see her in street clothes with her hair exposed. Generally, she did not go outside without a wig or at least a turban. Mother was going bald. It was not discussed. "Are we giving up drag to be a fuse person?"

"That would be an electrician, tiddles," Sitka snapped. "And no. I need to rename all the little tags before the plumber gets here. Seems wiring and water do not mix."

"Does that mean my darling little cupboard will be livable soon?!"

"Soon. Another month or two." My excitement died. "Such a pouty little bird face. The whole ceiling was ruined, the pipes were older than my first gaff—"

"Which you're still using no doubt."

"Don't be cheeky. It's framed and hanging in my bedroom. The whole mess was costly. So, I'm doing it little by little, which, as we all know, is the best way to do most things."

"Mm-hmm, so I hear. Do you need help? Can I fetch your bifocals or a magnifying glass?"

Her lips twitched. "You're such a disrespectful child. I'm fine. Go get changed and whatever you do, make sure that hulking boyfriend of yours does not block the bathrooms. Can't he sit at a table like he used to?"

"He felt too exposed," I replied with a sigh. Tyr had taken to hiding in the corridor with Eladio or perhaps in the dark recesses on the sides of the stage, just in case. Sitka gave me one of her long, sad looks. She didn't say diddly, though. She knew there was no point. I was committed to this relationship with Tyr. I loved him. No one knew that. Hell, I could barely confess it to my reflection in my makeup mirror for fear of it jinxing something. "I'll remind him to lean on the wall."

"If you ever wish to talk, you know where to find me." She kissed my brow, then returned to trying to read the old writing in the fuse box. With that sitting on my shoulders—why would I need to talk to her when everything was splendid with my Viking—I shoved my way into general population. The air in the dressing room was thick with perfume, dusting powder, and catty comments.

"…her hip pads were down to her ankles. I mean really, bitch. Gigi, pumpkin." Clarice blew me a kiss as I pattered behind her. I wiggled my fingers in reply.

"Are we talking about Monique?" I asked, then settled into my little space beside Jo-Jo. She passed me a packet of cheese crackers, which I politely waved off. Salty snacks made a body retain water. With the holiday shows right around the corner, every ounce counted.

"We were, then you came in with that dopey look on your face, so now I think we should talk about you and that big, bearded man that's making you walk so funny," Jo-Jo teased. I threw a powder puff at her.

"Spreading her legs just like peanut butter," Clarice tossed out. Jo-Jo snorted loudly.

"Must be jelly, 'cause jam don't shake like that," Jo-Jo chimed in. I ignored all the salty queens. Mostly because I couldn't argue. Tyr was between my legs every chance he got.

"You're all just jealous," I replied as I wiggled my electric razor out of my tote. "And wish you came moseying in here looking like you just got off a brahma bull."

The others all cackled in glee. It was always like this when Monique wasn't here. Laughter and sisterhood, reading each other, clucking like hens, just having fun. The chitchat went from my lover to other topics that ranged from eyeshadow to politics. No topic was off-limits, and no tea was missed. I was applying the final touches to my face ninety minutes after I'd started, which was my typical paint time, when I heard a rap on the door. It was distinctive. Five short knocks. Tyr was here.

I sprang from my stool, then bounced to the door, the taunts from my sisters falling on deaf ears. I did flip them off right before I cracked the door, though, just because. Tyr stood in the hall, beret in hand, saddle leather eyes roaming all over my tuxedo jacket and short shorts costume. Add a top hat and I was dressed exactly like Judy in *Summer Stock.*

"You look amazing," he said, then leaned in for a quick peck. He always blushed when we kissed in front of Eladio. Then, he would drag his thumb over his lips to remove the lipstick.

"Flatterer." I did look good, though. My legs were to fucking die for, and I was just exuding old Hollywood glamour. "Is everything okay?" I asked when he sighed. "You sound downcast."

"Just...nothing. We'll talk after the show. Hockey stuff."

Someone behind me laughed aloud. "Okay, well, find your stool. I'm due on stage in thirty."

"Okay." He looked as if he had something he wanted to say, but he just ambled off to the bar for his usual glass of Sprite. I watched him walk off, my eyes darting to his delicious skater's ass, then to Eladio who was shaking a finger at me. I flipped him off, as well.

I fiddled around backstage, sipping on a bottle of spring water as I waited for my cue from Sitka. When she opened the door, now dressed in a purple caftan with yellow polka dots as big as her head, I touched up my makeup and clip-clopped out behind her. Tyr was seated beside Eladio.

"I dare say, this pay for one, buy get two bouncers is good for my payroll expenses," Sitka flung over her shoulder.

I snuggled into Tyr's side. "I think she's starting to come around," I said while Sitka climbed onto the stage. I peeked around Tyr but could see little back here other than the bar was mobbed. Sunday nights were funny. They could be busy, or it could be dead. Tonight seemed to be another full house. Mother would be so pleased. He held me close, relatively at ease with Eladio and the other queens hustling around. Mostly at ease. Hidden among the shadows. His jaw was set, his attention elsewhere. I wanted to ask, but he wouldn't get into what kind of hockey stuff had happened with other people around.

"Maybe if I just offer to work for free for eternity, she'll start to accept me," he stated, his gaze dropping down to me.

"It would be a good start," I teased. It was nice to see a weak smile on his kissable mouth. "Free labor would tickle the old bean."

He pressed a kiss to my lips. Just a butterfly soft smooch so not to smudge my lipstick. Bless him, he was learning. That was when a gaggle of giggling women stumbled into the corridor. Tyr stiffened. I moved closer staking a claim, my arms around his waist.

"Tyr?" one of the pack of women asked, pushing around several drunken chippies to step closer. It was the blonde woman. The one who had been here with him that first night that the fates had brought us into the same space.

"Janine," Tyr gasped. He moved away from me instantly. I winced as if someone had pushed a blade between my ribs. The distance he'd hurried to place between us was a moot point, for Janine had seen us cuddling close. Hell, the bitch had probably seen him kissing me.

"Okay, well, this explains why you never wanted to crawl into *my* bed," she sniped, her words icy and clipped.

"It's not like that, I just..." He simply stopped talking as we both—Janine and I—were giving him seriously dank looks. She for her reasons, and me for mine. I was sure they were not the same reasons, but both were really quite justified. For some asinine reason, I assumed he would not shove me away as if I were a leper the first time someone he knew showed up. Stupid, lovesick fool that I am. Ugh. God, I felt scummy. As if I were a shameful secret.

You are, henny.

I heard my stage name being called. The crowds all rose and clapped. Janine stormed off, leaving her tipsy friends in the lurch. Tyr gave me a look that just about gutted me, then ran off after her. Bile rose up my throat. I swallowed several times and shivered at the sudden chill surrounding me. Tears threatened, but I blinked them away. Eladio's expression was pitiful. I was pitiful. A pitiful, stupid queen who should have known better. Mother had tried to tell me.

"Oh, baby girl." I cringed when Monique's voice forced its way into my ear.

"Do not even right now," I snapped. She threw her arms around me. My spine stiffened. Was the bitch going to shank me?

"Men are such bastards. I swear I hate every one of them," she said while patting my back in a consoling manner. I'd never knew the whore had an ounce of empathy within her desiccated heart. "Imagine giving you the ice. Fucker. Who needs him? Let him get back to his beard." She pulled back to look at me and I could have sworn I saw sympathy in her gaze. Had I been sucked into an upside-down bizarro universe? "You just take all the time you need. I'll go on for you."

"No, I'm good." As if I were letting her take my spot. Please, bitch.

She patted my face. "That's a girl. Tell that beret wearing cowardly queer to go back to Het-Land. We don't need his type around here."

"Right. Thanks." I swallowed down the keen of anguish that was right at the surface. What a dipshit I'd been. Of course, when push came to motherfucking shove, he ran after the bitch. Of course, he did. She was his ticket to the normal world. I was just the shameful hidden thing he stashed in a dark jar under the bed. God, I really felt skanky. Skanky and used. Like an old Kleenex. God, maybe Sitka had been right all along.

Stop it. Right now. You two are strong. He'll text you soon and tell you all is well. Life is fine. Fuck, do not cry, girl. Save it for later. The show must go on.

"You're on, Gigi," Eladio whispered. I nodded, threw my chin up and my shoulders back, and marched to the stage like a trooper. Judy would have done no less. Sitka met me at the stairs leading to the stage, her face tight.

"Do not even start," I told my mother, then found my spotlight as the club filled with thunderous applause.

Chapter Thirteen

TYR

MY WORLD WAS SO FRACTURED, SO RIFE WITH UPHEAVAL, I almost missed catching up with Janine. I'd gone left when she had, it appeared, gone right. After racing around a city block in a blind panic, I rounded the corner and nearly bowled her and her girlfriends over. They were all huddled on a street corner, ranks closed, talking at Janine all at once.

When I bounced off the streetlight, several feminine heads craned in my direction. One of them hissed. Like a real hiss that they used to throw at villains in silent movies. My gut clenched. What had Janine told them in my short absence? Had she revealed my secret? What if they went home and told their men? What then?

Then you're toast.

"Janine, can we talk?" I asked, my words fogging in front of me. I didn't sound like me at all. My fear made me sound as if I were speaking underwater.

The girls surrounding her began throwing nastiness my way. Janine nudged a tall brunette aside and closed the distance between her and I. I'd never been so terrified in all my life.

"Let's go to the diner," she said in a voice that was far too calm. I nodded. Her friends protested, but she waved them off. "It's fine. Go home." There was a short argument, but Janine was firm. The others slowly walked off, but the glowers that were flying my way were lethal. "Come on. I'm freezing." She pulled her fluffy coat up around her red ears. I nodded, unsure of what to say. She led, I fumbled along, my head unable to clear the chaotic chorus of terror swirling inside my skull. We didn't speak as we walked. Probably, we were both internalizing what had just happened.

The diner was an old railcar eatery that sat on the corner. It had been redone inside, retrofitted, and now looked just as it had back in the fifties. People said it was quaint and cute. Nostalgic. I'd been there a few times but found the food to be greasy and overly priced. Yet into Winnie's Diner we went. Janine chose an empty booth back by the doors to the kitchen. She removed her coat, tossed it to the bench, then shimmied into her seat. I stood with my hat in my hand.

"Sit down, Tyr, I'm not going to bite."

I wedged myself into the too small space, the edge of the table digging into my gut. A waitress in a red dress uniform with white apron appeared.

"Two coffees," Janine said as she thumbed a strand of blonde hair from her face. Her nails were pink, the same tone that Eli had worn last week. I yanked my sight from her hands to stare at my own hands. Scarred, the knuckles cracked, my nails blunt. "Thank you."

Two cups of dark as Hell coffee were placed in front of

us. The waitress, possibly sensing the impending upset, made herself scarce, wiping off the long counter as we sipped and sat in gut-wrenching silence.

"Go me for ruining Margo's promotion party," she sighed. I shrank in on myself a bit. "How long have you known you were gay?" Janine asked while stirring some Stevia into her coffee. I blinked away the tears that welled up. Then, because it was habit, I looked around the diner. It was late so the place was pretty quiet. One dude at the counter eating pie, talking with the waitress. A cook in the back, singing along to the radio in Spanish. Could that guy at the counter hear me if I confessed to being gay? "Hey."

A bright pink nail tapped the back of my hand. My spoon clattered to the speckled linoleum tabletop.

"Sorry, I'm just…"

"I'm not going to tell anyone, if that's what you're so scared about." I glanced up from my spoon lying half on my napkin and half off. She smiled. It was a precarious smile, but it did help to unwind the crippling fear crushing my windpipe. "I promise. I will not out you. I just…I want to know if you knew you were into men when you first asked me out."

"Yes," I croaked, my sight darting from the burst of pain in her blue eyes. I pushed my cup aside, then leaned over the table, the metal edge gouging my sternum. "I'm incredibly sorry for using you that way. I do like you. You're smart and friendly."

"No, no, it's…" She blew out a breath that made her cheeks billow like sales in a strong wind. "You don't have to apologize. Honestly, I get it. It hurts, is all. I feel like an idiot. I should have seen the signs when we were dating. Four months, Tyr. Four months we dated. I was starting to think that we were getting serious. That maybe you were being so kind and conscientious because you were so shy. That's why I never pushed, you know, for sex. I never grabbed your dick or anything because you were so backward around women. I found it endearing. I was such a fool."

"No, you weren't. I led you along. This is all on me, Janine."

"Did you sleep with that drag queen?" My eyes flared. "Sorry, no. Don't answer that. It was terrible of me to ask. I just…" She waved a hand in the air. "I'm just reeling. Although, I really shouldn't be. I should have sensed something was wrong. Now that I think on it, there were signs."

"I kept them deeply buried. Those signs. It wasn't until Eli that I couldn't keep the emotions and yearnings chained."

She pursed her lips, then blew over her coffee. "You shouldn't have to chain those feelings."

"I play hockey for a living. My window of getting into the pros is growing smaller. I'm twenty-five now. I should have been called up already. They keep saying I need a little more maturity, a little more honing. What will they say if they find out that I'm not into women? What will my teammates say? We trust each other. On the ice and off. What will they all do when they find out that I've been lying to them for the past three years? I cannot imagine what kind of explosion that would cause in the dressing room."

"But, Tyr, and I'm saying this as a friend." She lowered her cup to the matching saucer as a cop car raced by, reds and blues flashing, siren off. "You look really good."

I snorted. "Thank you. And how did I look before?"

"No, I'm not being a bitch. You do. There's a joy to you that was lacking before. Also, I need to apologize for that leg image. My God." She buried her face into her hands. "I sent a hootchie shot to a gay man."

"I couldn't see your hootchie, just your thigh. A lot of thigh." My mouth and throat were parched so I took a sip of coffee. It was incredibly strong and seared my tongue and throat. The coffee did nothing to settle my hyped nerves, but it was either drink or scream at the heavens. Drinking seemed the better of the two. "I am happy, for the most part."

"Really? You don't look happy right now. You look miserable and terrified."

"I'm scared that you're going to out me. I'm scared that someone else will out me. I'm scared that I'll be sent to Chicago and I'm scared that I won't. I'm scared of letting my father down…of not living…not living up to…what he…the dreams he had. I let my mother die. I didn't take care of her like he asked and now…" I choked on the fears flowing out of my mouth like vomit. Coughing madly, I grabbed my napkin, coffee stained as it was, and covered my face with it. Tears fell freely. Words I had no control over spewed out of me. Janine patted my forearm, though the entire debasing breakdown. The napkin was soaked when I was finally able to gather myself enough to lower it.

"Jesus, you were holding in a lot of shit. That's not good. As a health care provider and a friend—we are still friends, right?" I bobbed my head as I wiped at my face. Fuck, that was the single most embarrassing moment in my life. I was sure the waitress and the pie man were staring at me as if I'd sprouted a second head. "Good. I want us to be friends. As your friend, and the only friend that you have who knows about you and Eli?" I nodded once more, blew my nose, and then shoved the napkin into my pocket. "Wow, you really are carrying a lot. Okay, so as a health care provider and your friend." She reached over the table to take my hand. Her fingers slid between mine with ease. I chanced a glance. Her gaze was warm, caring, and lacking any judgement. "I suggest you take some time to work out this issue. It's not healthy to live in such denial of your true self."

"I know, but—"

"No. No buts." She shook her head. "Is there anyone you can talk to? A team counselor?"

"Yeah, probably, but if I tell him, then who's to say he won't tell the team? I have to make it to the pros."

"Why?"

"Because…" I drew up short for a second. Obviously, my mind was a mess. There were lots of reasons to enter the pros. "Cash, prestige, love of the game. It was what my father asked of me on his death bed."

"Well, you can love the game and play in the minors. Cash, sure, that's nice. Prestige is fleeting. I just…" She twisted her lips. "I guess I just don't see why you feel this compulsion to force yourself to do something that someone else felt you needed to do. I get that it was a dad thing, but, Tyr, you're not happy. Even with a guy that you really like—and I can tell you adore him. The look you had when you were holding him close…You never looked at me like that."

"I'm sorry." I drank more coffee.

"Don't be sorry. I totally get it. And now that I know

why you never found me attractive in that way, my ego can heal."

"You're very pretty. And kind."

"You told me that already."

"It needs to be repeated."

"Well, I'm always happy to hear how pretty I am." She preened then flipped her hair. "Seriously, though, you need to come to grips with who you are, where you want to go, and who you want to make that trip with. If it's Eli, then you're going to have to make some big changes. But I think they'd be changes for the better, don't you?"

"Hockey is all I know…all I have."

She squeezed my fingers lightly. "I don't think that's true anymore, is it?"

That brought me up short. "But my father…"

"Is dead. And I'm super sorry about his passing, but you have to live your life the way *you* want. We can't exist merely to carry out the wishes of others. Maybe your calling is something else, some other career."

"I have no skills outside of hockey."

"I find that hard to believe. You went to college. What was your major?"

"Creative writing." God, I could still hear my father's rage over that, but then my mother reminded him that what I studied wasn't important. My real love was hockey, and that would never change. Besides, she was a poet and could help ensure I didn't flunk out, which would keep me in the hockey program. Papa finally relented. It was the one and only time that my mother had fought for me and my silly fables. Perhaps it was the only way she could encourage me to create something with words as she once had. Before her marriage, before her mental illness overtook her.

"There you go. Maybe you can be the next Stephen King." I scoffed into my coffee mug. "It's a possibility. You're allowed to change your mind about your life, Tyr."

"I know."

"Hmm, you say that, yet I wonder if you really do. I'm worried about you now. Before I was mad and hurt, but now…well, now I'm concerned. Will you promise me that you'll *think* about talking to someone other than me or your new boyfriend? He's so pretty. I need him to teach me how to apply eyeliner like he does."

"He'd show you. He's really sweet. Sassy. I like him."

She grinned at me. "I can tell. Did you and he start dating that night we all went to the club?"

One question was all it took for the floodgates to open. We had another cup of coffee as I yammered on and on about Eli, and Gigi, and the club and fables. When I ran out of steam and Janine was yawning, it was well past two in the morning.

"Let me call you a ride," I offered after we'd paid for our coffee and left a tip. Patting myself down, I realized that I didn't have my phone. I took a moment to think and recalled that I'd snuck a quick text to Eli after the game. I'd laid it on the shelf in my cubicle, then had been beset with reporters and a long, dismal talking to from Coach. Ugh, that game. I'd played terribly. How was I going to ever get the call from Chicago if I kept screwing up? "I left my phone at the barn."

"It's fine." She made the call. I helped her into her coat, then waited just inside the vestibule with her until her Uber pulled up. "I'm glad we ran into each other. I feel much better. I hope you do, too." I nodded, my beret slipping down a bit. "Good. Listen, if you ever want to talk, you have my number."

"I do, yes. Thank you for being so understanding." I shook her hand.

She went to her tiptoes to kiss my cheek. Then she smiled at me. "Go be happy, Tyr. You deserve to live the life that *you* want to live."

"Yes, thank you. I'll work on that." I escorted her to her ride then watched as it pulled off. A chilly rain began to fall. Tugging my beret down and my collar up, I hustled back to Campo Royale, eager to see Eli and explain. He'd looked devasted. I'd have some big apologizing to do, but he would understand.

My face was cold when I tugged on the front doors of the club. Locked. Damn it. I raced around back and was met at the employees' entrance by Monique. She was alone, out of drag, and pissed, if her dark looks meant anything.

"We're closed. Go on back to your girlfriend," Monique snapped, giving me a shove. I grabbed onto the cold, damp brick as the door was slammed in my face. That made me angry. I hammered on the door with both hands. "You keep that up and I *will* call the cops!"

Fuck. I lowered my fists to my sides. "I need to see Eli."

"Gigi is all done with your cheating ass, so you best crawl back to your beard."

"What?" My fingers unclenched as a cold dread settled in my stomach. "No, he wouldn't just end it like that," I told the door and the man behind it. He wouldn't. We loved each other. I'd not said it yet, didn't dare, for if I told him how much I cared then had to leave…

"That is where you're wrong. Eli doesn't date fans. He only fucks them. Guess your drama outweighed his appreciation of your dick. So be a good hetero and go back to your girl."

I let my brow drop to the door. Hard. I had fucked it up. "I just need to talk to him."

"Go on. Hide that fag deep down inside and get moving before I call the po-po. Imagine how good that will look when they bust your ass outside a drag club. I can see the headlines now! Queer ass hockey player arrested outside Campo Royale after altercation with police. Witnesses say the big sissy star was wailing and beating on the door of the above-named establishment begging to see the queen he'd been fucking in the ass."

I choked back a curse, then spun and slogged to my car parked down the block. All I could think of was to go to Eli's home. I knew where he lived. We'd talk it out. He'd been hurt, yes, I'd seen that in his dark eyes, but he would understand. He'd be happy that Janine was cool. Monique was probably lying. Eli would see me. I knew he would. God, he *had* too.

Chapter Fourteen

ELI

I WAS SUPER TEMPTED TO JUST LET HIM STAND OUT THERE IN the cold.

If I had an ounce of sense, I would have. He'd grow tired of rapping on my door eventually, and I could mope to my heart's content. I'd have three hours alone with Madame Rocky Road. I was already dipping into her creamy chocolate, nutty, marshmallowy deliciousness. I'd have this gallon polished off before Hank got home, then I would weep on his shoulder. Maybe he would beat-up Tyr, if he were still here. Big brothers did that sort of thing all the time. I'd just tell him that Tyr had treated me like a used condom and PUNCH!

"Eli, I see you standing there. You're in a green robe," Tyr called through the mail slot.

"It's seafoam," I whipped back, then shoveled another spoonful of ice cream into my face. "And stop spying on me! God, you sicko!"

"Sorry." The flap closed. Then he knocked again. "I see you look sad and are eating ice cream."

"No, I'm not," I replied around a mouthful of ice cream. The cold made my fillings ache. "I'm not sad. I'm glad. Glad! Glad! Glad! You finally showed me who was more important to you."

I heard his sigh through the door. "She is not more important to me than you are. Eli, please, let me in."

I huffed, stomped my foot, ate another shovelful of Rocky Road, and then finally threw the lock open.

"It's unlocked, but I'd come in slowly if I were you, because I am an irate, heartbroken queen with a weapon!" I shouted as the door creaked open. He stuck his head in, thankfully without that silly beret, and gave me a quick onceover. I shook my serving spoon in his face. "This is all the weapon I need."

"I'll be careful," he whispered, then slid inside, closing the door then resting his shoulder blades to the wood. "Thank you for talking to me."

"Whatever. I hate stupid movies where stupid people refuse to talk about their stupid problems to each other like stupid adults." He nodded enthusiastically. I saw his hat sticking out of the pocket of his brown coat and pointed at it with my spoon. "Toss that silly thing outdoors."

"My hat?" he asked, his sweet tea eyes widening.

"Yes. As an act of contrition." I licked my sticky lips. Bless his heart, the man actually opened the door then whipped his hat out into the darkness. "Okay, good. You passed that test."

"Can we sit down?"

"No. We're going to do this right here standing because I'm not sure if I wish to offer you access to anything in my house other than my foyer." He looked around. "I know it's not an actual foyer! Stop being so literal. Oh, my gods!"

"Sorry. I'll be less literal. I'm happy to be inside here to talk. Eli, tonight was not good."

"Mpfh mumming mpfh," I said, then swallowed. "You chose her over me."

"No, no, I didn't choose her over you." He shook his head violently, his lips flattening as he pulled up what he wished to say. "Eli, there is never going to be anyone I choose over you."

"Huh." I ate more ice cream, chewed a nut, then shifted some so my left hip popped out. He needed to see that hip leaning out, so he knew I meant fucking business.

"I'm serious."

"I'm not sure you are."

His shoulders fell. "I understand. Monique told me that you said you were done with my cheating ass but if you just let me explain to you—"

"*What?!* Oh, that botoxed ham-footed bitch. I never said that. Never! She was the one going on and on about what shits men are because you men *are* shits."

"You're a man, too," he pointed out. I flung a marshmallow at his handsome fucking face. It hit his cheek then fell to the carpet. "Sorry, I meant to say…" He rubbed at his face with a big hand. "I'm not sure what I'm saying anymore, other than my heart attempting to tell you that I love you. There is no one else for me. Janine is not you."

"Well, that's obvious. Have you seen her roots? I mean, bitch really, get a touch up." I spooned up yet another glob of Rocky Road when it sunk in. The ice cream melted in my mouth as I stood there staring up at the mountain of

Dane looking so utterly forlorn. "Did you just say you love me?"

"I did. I do. Madly."

That lowered my tiff. "Then why didn't you call me? Or text me? It's been at least four days since you ran after her."

"It's not been four days. It's been a few hours."

"It felt like four days." I sighed. "I'm being a little dramatic, aren't I?" He pinched some air between his fingers. "Ugh. Okay, let me gather myself." I ate more ice cream, like a serving spoon full. It was hard to fit it into my mouth, but I did it. Then, as my toes curled into the carpet from the choco/nut/mallow delightfulness, I shoved the carton into his chest. "Take this," I said as I chewed then swallowed. I licked my lips. His pupils grew fat. So, I did it again. He placed the ice cream on a side table and closed the distance between us. I stood my ground, head tipping up, as he moved in. His chest brushed mine. My dick was totally into this scenario.

"There will never be anyone for me other than you," he told me in a low, gummy sweet voice that sent tingles of want right to my taint. "I love you."

"I love you, too," I whispered, eyes tearing up slightly. "Next time one of your leggy ex's shows up, don't leave me stewing in my juices for hours. Text me!"

"I would have, but my phone must be in my locker at the barn. I ran to the club as soon as we were done talking. She said—"

I placed two fingers over his lips. "I don't care what she said. Oh, well, okay, yes I do, but only in the context of whether she was going to keep our secret." He nodded then sucked my index finger into his mouth. That was pretty much all it took for my cock to rise to attention in my joggers. Yes, I was doing fleece and feathers. Judge not, lest you be judged or something like that. There was a blaze burning in his gaze. I shuddered at the sight. "Good for her. I would hate to have to kick her ass. Monique is already in line for an ass kicking of…oh God. Tell me you love me again."

He let my finger slide from between his lips. I melted into his arms, pressing us together, chest to toes, his hard cock poking my belly.

"I love you. Only you. Forever."

"Same. Same. Same!" I jumped up, threw my arms around his neck and slammed my mouth to his. His growl vibrated through me as our tongues tangled. My fingers fisted in his hair as he hoisted me from the floor. My legs went around his waist. He bumbled and bounced off walls and furniture as we made our way to my bed. I sucked a dark mark on his neck, just in case some other bimbo beard showed up in the next week or so.

We crashed into my dresser before we fell onto the bed. Clothes were quickly shed. A condom was rolled over his huge prick as I worked some slick up into my ass. Then, finally, we were skin-to-skin. He moved over me, into me, filling me, stretching me, pounding into me with a fervor that made me howl in pleasure. We rolled over the bed, my knee finding the lube bottle as I saddled up and rode him hard. He worked more lube around my hole as I bounced up and down on his cock. My cock bounced, slapping his belly. He spread my cheeks wider and wider, his slick fingers touching his prick as it slid in and out.

"I love…makeup sex!" I shouted right before my

asshole clamped around him as I coated his hairy belly and chest with cum.

"Close...so close," he snarled as jets of spunk flew from me. He grabbed my hips, his grip punishing, and held me down as he rocked upward. His dick pulsed as he filled the condom. My fingers bit into his pecs, smearing pearly droplets into his chest hair. He bucked hard, but I rode that bull for the whole eight seconds plus. Tyr slid a hand down over his chest, then carried my cum to his mouth. Eyes glowing like embers, he licked his fingers clean. "You're delicious."

"I love you," I gasped then lay down on him, plastering my mouth to his, lapping at his molars to pick up the taste of my seed. Cum spread between us like paste.

"I love you as well," he panted into my mouth. We kissed forever, touching each other all over, until he had to move to tend to the condom. With him at my back, we showered, the water slightly too hot for me but I was unwilling to move. His lips travelled over my wet skin, gliding over every hairless inch, until he was sucking on my cock as water sluiced down over us. Back flat to the tiles, I pumped leisurely in and out of his mouth, easing more and more of my cock into his throat. He gagged and groaned, his hands on my ass, feeding him dick until I blew apart. He coughed and swallowed, kneading my thighs as I pounded on the wall.

"Good God," I huffed before I was swept up in his arms then carted back to bed.

"Can we...I wanted to ask if...my last physical was clear. Everything was negative. Could we...if you want?"

"Oh, shit yes, I want so much. I'm negative, too. I take

PrEP and always used condoms. Please, yes, I want to feel you fill me up."

He groaned deep and low, then nudged my legs wide. Two fat fingers slippery with lube slid into me. Eyes closed, I writhed and rolled, begging for his cock over and over until he withdrew his fingers and lined up the deep red head of his prick with my eager hole. His eyes rolled back when he pressed into me. I clawed at his shoulders, arching up the best I could to make sure I had every heavenly inch. Then, he plowed me into the mattress. When his second orgasm rode down on him, I cradled his face, my knees by his shoulders, and forced him to stare at me as he came. Something metaphysical passed between us as he pumped jet after jet into me. It was like our minds and souls joined in a cosmic collision. Or something deeply profound like that. Fucked if I knew what formed between us at that moment. I did know it was powerful and life altering. Maybe the planets had realigned, or the earth tipped on its axis. Maybe it was just two men finally letting down their barriers so that love could flow into and over them.

"Love you," he huffed, burying his face into my neck as my legs slipped down off his broad shoulders to the mattress. The sheets and blanket had been rucked off in our passion. "Thank you for…everything. Loving me back. I never thought I could have this…be so happy."

My heart swelled. I held him close, sensing he needed a good hug. And several hundred kisses. He gently withdrew amid touches and caresses. I couldn't keep my hands to myself, nor could he. We cleaned up, again, then crawled into my bed. Lying facing each other, the covers resting by our ears, we lay there with just the glow of a small lamp to see by. His face was a masterpiece of masculinity. I could stare at him for hours, days, weeks.

"My life is so crazy outside these walls," he softly said as his sight dipped to my puffy lips. I could feel the chafing from his kisses, as well as the burn of his possession. "But when I'm here, with you, all seems right with the world. I wish we could be out together. Hiding it is wearing me down."

"We will be. You'll see. I knew what I was getting into. I'm happy to wait until you get that call. Then, when you're a big star, we can be a couple. A proud, gay couple that the world will envy."

A sleepy smile danced on his lips. I stole one final taste before my eyes drifted shut. My dreams were all cotton candy, butterflies, and unicorns. Then my phone started ringing. I flopped to my side. My arm fell over a snoring Viking. Sitting up, lost and bleary-eyed, I shimmied over Tyr to fetch my phone on the bedstand. It was my brother. It was also five in the fucking morning. Oh. My. God. What the *hell* was he doing calling me at this hour? He knew I needed my beauty sleep, or I got cranky.

"Hank, I swear, unless this is a life and death matter, I am not even going to speak to you in English." I grumbled in a made-up language.

"Cool, was that Dothraki or Klingon?" Hank asked. Tyr mumbled sleepily then rolled away from me, his back bared to my sight. He had massive shoulders that needed to be kissed. I yawned, too tired to even pucker.

"It was angry queen. What's up?"

"What do you mean, 'What's up?' Tyr hasn't told you?"

I glanced at the slumbering behemoth in my bed. "No."

I rubbed at my eyes with my fingers, phone pinched between ear and shoulder.

"Oh. Well, tell him to turn on his phone. He's there, right?"

"Yes, but he's sleeping."

"Not anymore," Tyr grumbled as he moved to his back, one thick arm dropping over his eyes. "What's up?"

A soft little warning buzzer began to sound in my head. "Hank says you need to turn on your phone."

"It's in my locker." He sat up, weaved back and forth, and scrubbed at his face with his hands. "Can he just tell us what's going on?"

"Morgan Booth was injured in a game against Dallas," Hank gushed.

"You woke me up to tell me that some guy named Morgan Booth was injured in a—hey!" I squeaked when Tyr removed the phone from my hand without even asking. "Rude!" All the sleepiness had left his face. The buzzer was chiming louder now. "What's going on? Who is Booth Morgan? What do we care if he got hurt? Tyr? What's going on?"

I pulled the covers up to my chin. My room suddenly felt chilly and damp. Tyr left my bed, thanking my brother for the call, then began punching at my cell.

"Tyr? Please, what is going on?" I was scared now.

"Morgan Booth is the star center for the Mules." He paced and punched. My gaze moved over his legs, the muscles bunching and releasing as he moved. Why was he so agitated? What did some guy in Chicago suffering from an injury have to do with us? "Shit. Okay, wow." He dropped to the edge of the bed with my phone. I scurried closer to read over his shoulder. We watched a video. A man in a red jersey was crunched by a man in a green jersey. The man in the red jersey hit his head on the boards. Hard. So hard he went down like a marionette with its strings cut. And there he lay on the ice, unmoving. I buried my face into Tyr's shoulder, unable to watch anymore. I prayed to whoever that Tyr would never get crunched that badly.

"Is he dead?" I asked.

"No, but he's out. Upper body injury, the sports pages are saying, but that's a concussion, for sure. They're already out a winger. They'll call someone up." I lifted my nose from his shoulder. He glanced back at me. "Can I call Coach?"

"Yes, of course," I replied in a timid little field mouse voice. I snuggled into his back, wrapping the cover around us, inhaling his scent from his skin. The call to his coach was short and succinct. The warning buzzer was now an air raid siren. Tyr blew out a breath. I pressed a kiss to his spine, right between the sharp blades straining his flesh. "They've called me up. I have to meet the plane at New Castle Airport at nine so I can be on the ice for the game against Philly tonight."

He looked back. I bit down on my bottom lip. "Yay?" I said as he reached back to pull me into his lap. His nose found my collarbone. I wrapped my arms around him tightly. "Love me one more time before you leave? Do you have time?"

"Always. For you, I always have time."

He left an hour later, sneaking out into the pink-purple of predawn to fly off to live his dream. Minus me.

Chapter Fifteen

TYR

I DROVE HOME IN A DAZE.

The sole thing that I'd been living for since I was old enough to store memories had just happened. I'd been called up to the pros. Where was the elation?

Rain speckled my windshield, the wipers torpidly removing the fat drops. Pulling up to a red light, I searched my heart to find the excitement that I should be feeling. Digging deep, I finally found it. It was buried under the sadness of leaving Eli. Shouldn't I be more jazzed? This was the moment. The pinnacle. Tonight, I would skate on ice in a pro jersey. The light flipped to green. I eased off the brake and turned toward the barn. I had to get my phone before I went home. Security greeted me at the player's entrance with claps on the back and well wishes. Jogging into the Warthogs dressing room, I paused to drink it all in. Would I ever come back to Wilmington? How long would I be gone? My father would be horrified if he could read my thoughts. What would we do, Eli and I, if I never came back? Would he come to

Chicago and live with me? How could that happen when I wasn't out?

I emptied out my cubicle in silence, taking a moment to check my phone. Messages and texts flowed in and the team chat was already humming with shoutouts from the other Warthogs. Smiling as I read over the congratulations and playful taunts to not come back, I noted that Ben was silent. Could be he wasn't awake yet but that was doubtful. Morning skate was now in two hours. Fuck. I had two hours!

I raced home, shocked to find Dante parked in my spot. I'd not seen him off the ice in weeks. I pulled up behind him. We hugged it out on the sidewalk, cold winter rain sending us indoors with haste.

"What the hell are you doing here?" I asked as we climbed the stairs to my place.

"I've been trying to contact you since the news about Booth hit the wires last night. Man, she must be a fucking tornado in bed if you're not picking up my calls."

I grimaced and sighed internally. "I left my phone in my locker."

"Uh-huh," he teased, slapping my shoulder while I unlocked my door. "Whatever your poor excuse, I wanted to see you before you flew off to the Windy City, never to return."

"I'll be back. It's just to fill in." Still, now that it had been said out loud, a shot of adrenalin coursed through me. Not enough to hide the ache of kissing Eli goodbye for who knew how long, but thankfully, there was some excitement now.

"That's what Jeremy Doe said last year, remember?" I nodded. Yeah, I did remember. And Jeremy was still in

Chicago playing for the Mules, making the big money and living the life Papa had yearned for. It could be mine, now. It was within my grasp. But at what cost? "They'll make a permanent spot for you, just wait and see. It's your time to shine, buddy!"

I smiled at him. "I hope so."

"Ah, stop being so damn humble. If anyone deserves this chance, it's you. So, what are you taking with you?"

I had no idea. Somehow, we managed to fill a couple of suitcases with clothes and personal items. While we whipped stuff into bags, Dante chattered away steadily, which helped to ease my growing nerves. He was in the closet going through my suits. I'd need at least one, maybe two. Did I have two suits?

"Something you want to tell me?" I glanced up from jamming socks into my suitcase to see Dante cradling a garter belt. A red one. A red, personalized one that had GIGI spelled out in rhinestones. Eli had flung them into the air last week during an impromptu strip tease number. We'd not been able to find the missing garter the next morning. Obviously, it had flown into the cracked closet door. Shit. Shit. All joy fled instantly. *Fuck.*

"It's mine." He cocked an eyebrow. The lacy red belt would barely span my wrist, let alone one of my thighs. "A memento of the night we went to that drag bar."

He hung the garter belt on the doorknob, his gaze unreadable. My heart was thundering in my chest so hard, drawing in a breath was nearly impossible.

"Okay, if that's what you're going with, I'll play along." He pulled a gray jacket and matching slacks off a hanger then flung it at me. I caught it, then nervously rolled it into a ball. His sight held mine. "Look, I know there are things that we all hide away from other people for whatever reasons we might have. I get it. And if you're not ready yet to tell me about…whatever it is that you hide, then cool. I'm not going anywhere. When you're ready to share or just want to talk, I'll be here. Or maybe I'll be in Chicago as well!"

"I…thank you." He nodded and went back into my closet to rummage through my meager selection of ties. I could barely swallow. Had he just said what I think he said? That he suspected my secret and was okay with it? Did I dare dip my toes into the waters of honesty? "Gigi is…special."

He peeked around the doorjamb, five ugly ties around his thick neck. "Yeah? I'm glad. I kind of figured there was a special friend. What else would explain the stupid smile on your face or the lack of downtime spent with your best friend?" He padded over to lay the ties on my bed as I tried to stamp down the guilt now clawing to life. That callout was accurate. I'd not spent any time with Dante since Eli had come into my life. All my time off was now spent with my boyfriend, hiding at his place or mine or at the club where I lurked. Hidden. In the shadows. "Hey, it's cool," he added when I remained silent. "The first six months with Maya, I saw nothing but the barn and her bedroom."

We shared a long look. "I'm not ready yet for everyone to know about my friendship with Gigi."

"I got that. Just know that I'm very cool with it. And if you ever feel ready to tell people about Gigi and your friendship, I'll be right at your side. Might have to fly to Chicago to stand there, but I'll be there."

Speaking was dicey. "Thank you." I reached out for a

hand. He slapped his palm over mine. It was more of a hand hold than a shake, but it tore me to bits inside. My phone vibrated. I coughed and let go of his hand to see what was happening now. "Fuck. It's the car the team sent to take me to the airport."

Dante's eyes rounded. We finished packing in two minutes flat. As I was bolting out the door, coat and laptop under my arm, I paused just outside my door.

"There's an extra key in the dish by the TV. Will you come over and water my plants until I get home?"

"You're not coming back to this town." He grabbed the back of my neck, then pulled me close for a quick, awkward hug. "Be great. Knock heads. Be you. You got me?"

"Yeah, I got you." We parted, his smile a sad one. A horn tooted.

"Go. Show them what a motherfucking berserker Viking can do." I nodded, then tore down the stairs and out into a chilly December morning. How I wished it would snow. Maybe there was snow already in Chicago. I missed white Christmases. A dark blue sedan was parked behind my car. The driver smiled and flashed a Mules ID badge at me as I neared the car. He took my bags. As he tossed them into the trunk, I gave my building a last look. Then, I turned my gaze in the direction of Eli's home. Thinking of him made me melancholy.

"Ready? Your flight leaves in less than an hour," the driver asked.

"Yes, let's do this."

FROM THE MOMENT my plane touched down at O'Hare, the day was bedlam. I was whisked to a hotel where I'd be staying for the foreseeable future. A really plush one. Not that I got to spend much time in my suite. I'd taken a short video to send to Eli, along with a note telling him that I missed him already and couldn't wait to see him again. He'd replied with kissy lip emojis, as well as oohs and aahs over the luxury accommodations. I had just enough time to splash some water on my face, grab a soda from the small fridge in the room, and change into a suit.

The driver who had picked me up at O'Hare was named Jimmy. The lanky Canadian who worked with the Mules organization was waiting for me in the lobby. When I came down, I was then carted to the Merry Morris Bank Arena in downtown Chicago. It was much, much colder here than in Wilmington. Snow was in the forecast and a wind that ripped flesh from bone blew in off the great lake. I tried to take in as much of the city as I could from the backseat of a Ford. I was suitably impressed and nervous as a pigeon in a cattery. It felt weird to be so happy about another man's misfortune. It was part of life in the world of hockey. Sometimes, the sport was grossly unfair to one while it offered another a once-in-a-lifetime opportunity. I had to make the most of it. For Papa. For Eli. For me. Even if I ended up back in Wilmington in a month or two, I had to give it my all.

We hustled through corridors that I would never be able to navigate without unspooling red thread like Theseus had to find his way out of the maze the Minotaur lived in. Norse was not the only mythology I enjoyed learning about.

"Did you have time to eat?" Jimmy asked as a new

notebook was placed into my hands. It would have all the plays I would need to learn. In three hours. My head spun at the thought.

"I'm not sure I can eat," I replied with candor.

He laughed. "That's normal. What do you feel like?"

"What do you suggest?" We finally arrived in the players area, the workout room with weights and bikes, massage rooms, skate sharpening room. Places that were the same no matter what barn you were in.

"A couple of jibarito's and a tossed salad. Maybe some milk?" Jimmy asked while steering me around men in shorts playing soccer. I recognized many of them and it seemed they knew of me as well, for they called out my name in greeting.

"Yes, sure?"

"You'll love a jibarito, trust me. This is the dressing room. All should be ready for you. If you have any questions, you can reach me at extension star 889. Good luck!"

He dashed away before I could thank him properly. My stomach growled as I thought of food. Then, I stepped into the Mules dressing room and all thought of sandwiches and salads took to wing. Several men were slowly getting geared up. They all glanced my way. I stopped dead right in front of the giant Mules logo on the red carpeting and let my eyes wander. Over the open lockers were nameplates. Above the nameplates was a pole with hangars. Situated over the poles were shelves filled with personal items. Above the shelves was a small expanse of wall that read:

"Excellence is not an exception; it is a prevailing attitude." ~ Colin Powell

I stared at that saying for a full minute as memories of late nights on the ice with my father threatened to overwhelm me. My sight found my name on a cubicle. Within that little open locker was my sweater. Bright red as an apple, it was, with HEMMINGSEN across the back over a large white 43. I took a picture, then flipped it over to show the braying mule logo on the front.

"Holy hell," I whispered, then startled when "Immigrant Song" blared to life from the old boombox sitting atop a plastic bin filled with stick tape. The guys in the room chuckled, then threw stinky socks at me. "Is this how you ward off a pillaging Viking?" I shouted as I tossed a sweaty, rolled-up sock into the air a few times. The men laughed, then one that I knew well from TV placed his book aside, got to his skates, and ambled over.

"Welcome to the Mules," Derry Knightly said as he offered me his hand. Derry was the captain of the team. Famous for his soft-spoken, stoic ways on and off the ice. He was an amazing player, second line center, and a future hall-of-famer.

"I am so pleased to be here," I tossed out and was swallowed up by hulking men in various stages of undress. The locker room was a warm, welcoming place. Handshakes and pats on the back. All quite friendly and brotherly.

"Get settled in and find a moment or two to absorb it. This is your first call-up, right?" I nodded, then quickly removed my beret and shoved it into my coat pocket. "Then definitely take a minute or two to soak it up. You need food? I know it can be frantic coming up unexpectedly."

"Jimmy was getting me something," I waved a hand at the doorway.

"Ah, good. Eat, read the plays, and most of all enjoy the night. Oh, and if you can toss that weight of yours around *and* score a goal, that would be great. No pressure, though." He winked, slapped my shoulder then went back to the book—a hardback book—he'd been reading when I'd entered. I followed the captain's advice. I drank it all in, then took more pictures of my sweater and sent it to Eli before posting on my dusty Instagram account.

I no sooner got my IG post sent when Eli hit me up in messenger.

E~ OMG! YOU HAVE A RED JERSEY WITH AN ASS ON THE FRONT!! I SO WANT ONE!!

A smile broke free. I turned from the men, sat down, and hunkered over my phone to reply to his manic message.

T~ Why are you yelling?

E~ BECAUSE I LOVE ASS! And I am so proud of you, baby.

A wave of emotion crashed down on me. I was proud of me, too. Yet, there were parts of me, huge parts, that I treated as shameful. I hated hiding the fact that I loved a man. It took a bit of the shimmer off what should be an amazing experience. I couldn't even tag Eli on social media in case someone saw me talking with a drag queen. What kind of way was that to live your life? Mired in a bog of fear, concealing your core self from others, wallowing in anxiety. It was no way to live a life. Something had to change.

E~ You still there?

T~ Yes! Always here for you. I was just...a little overwhelmed. I shook hands with Derry Knightly.

E~ Yaaaaaayyyyy!!

T~ You have no idea who he is, do you?

E~ Nary one idea. But he sounds gorge.

I chuckled. Fuck, but I loved this man.

T~ I miss you already.

E~ I miss you too. Hank says do not wash your hand. Knightly germs are precious like gold. Jocks are weird.

That made me snort. I rolled my shoulders. Tension was coiled inside me like a python.

"Hey, War God. Your mortal fare has arrived!" I looked up to see a slightly younger guy in a green coat holding a brown takeout bag. Beside him stood Mike Crenshaw, a Mules winger and owner of the fastest slapshot in last year's All-Star game. The delivery boys' eyes were round as dinner plates as he stared at the dressing room. I tried to pay the kid, but he said it was already paid for, so I dug into my wallet and gave him a nice tip. He then got my autograph, even though he had no clue who I was.

T~ Sorry. My lunch arrived.

E~ Go eat, lamb. I'm going to finish up the bead work I'm doing on my Christmas revue costume then watch you make goals.

E~ Then I have to go rehearse with the bitches.

E~ I hope Monique is there. I am going to clock that crusty cunt.

E~ Don't try to talk me out of it!

E~ She tried to break us up. The bitch is mine!

Fifteen slap emojis followed his text tirade. No one would ever say that Eli McBride was not exuberant. The smell of whatever kind of sandwich was in the bag tickled my nose. My gut roared.

T~ Be nice. It's nearly Christmas. I have to go. I love you and miss you.

E~ Ugh. Fine. I'll be nice THEN slap a crusty cunt. I love you too. Make a goal for me. Don't get crunched. XOXOXOXOXOXOXXO

I rubbed my thumb over the X's and O's, then shook off the sadness. This was a night to be celebrated. My first professional game. I rose from the black plastic bench, food in hand, and gave the jersey hanging in my temporary cubicle a caress.

"Jeg klarede det, Pappa."

Yes, I had made it. Wherever he was, I hoped he could rest peacefully, now. Perhaps I could now live the life that *Tyr* wished to lead. The vow had been fulfilled. My life *had* to change. I had to break free. If that meant giving up a hand to Fenrir, then that was what I would do. I could do no less than my namesake had.

Chapter Sixteen

ELI

"Do you think either one of you could manage to stop watching the pregame show and help me trim the tree?"

I looked from my white muff to Becky glaring at us manly men on the sofa.

"I'm not watching the pregame show, I'm beading my muff." I held up the fluffy ivory hand warmer. It was an essential part of my holiday ensemble for the Christmas show and each white bead had to be handsewn into place. It was boring, tedious work, but would be ab fab when the spotlight hit me for my solo. Think Rosemary Clooney's red Mrs. Santa dress from "White Christmas," only with more tits and ass for Bing-A-Ling to ogle over.

"Maybe if I beaded *my* muff, my boyfriend would pay attention to me," Becky flung back. Hank's dark eyes flittered from the screen to his girl waiting beside the fake tree we'd lugged down from the crawlspace. He was the epitome of relaxed straight dude, right down to his left hand resting inside the waistband of his Warthogs fleece pants.

"I have a merkin you can borrow. Un-beaded, of course, but I do have holiday beads!" I waved my bead box in the air.

"Don't bead your muff, babe. I'll get a loose bead up my ass when we're in bed."

"Oh! I have those kinds of beads, too," I added as I returned to pulling thread through muff. "Tyr loves the sparkly pink ones."

"That is *way* too much information," Hank replied after a dramatic gag or two. Becky huffed. He sighed and pushed to his feet. "Shout when the game starts."

I folded my legs into a lotus and nodded.

"You're five feet from the screen," Becky pointed out as they began placing store bought ornaments from several Dollar Bonanza bags.

This was the first year Hank and I had put up a tree. There hardly seemed any point before. Our parents didn't bother to call or visit. No. That's not true. They mailed packages to Hank. None for me. Whatever. That only hurt tremendously, but so what, he said as he stabbed a needle into a muff. Hank always got pissed about that slight and shipped all the presents back. Then, they fought on the phone. Over me. So yeah, that was one reason we were like, "Fuck the X and Mass" the past few years.

Also, Hank usually worked for the double time pay on Christmas and I was on the road doing a show or pageant. This year, though, we both had someone special in our lives. Also, Becky had made us. She's sweet as pie but quite bossy at times. Like now.

They hung little doves and snowmen on the slightly crooked tree while two old Canadian men, ex-hockey players I had to assume, prattled on and on about Tyr being called up. My gosh, they were as hot for him as I was, and that was saying something, because I loved that man of mine! Hell, I didn't gush about him like Frick and Dick did. Then again, I really couldn't gush about him to anyone other than Hank and Becky. It sucked, to be honest. I wanted to parade around the club in one of his jerseys and rub my romance into certain pinched faces. Shit, I'd tell the motherfucking world that Eli was in love with Tyr! But I didn't dare. I sighed and beaded. It was fine. I knew what I was getting into with this relationship. Mother had warned me about dating fans, and jocks, and closeted homosexuals, and men with tacky shoes, and circus performers. Seemed she had a bad romance with a clown once. Mother had a warning for all her daughters about every type of male on the planet. You'd think she wanted us to only date other drag queens, but she was also against a good kai-kai. Mother simply didn't trust men.

I glanced up from my muff. There were men on the ice. Burly men in red jerseys. "They're making sport!" I shouted, then cursed as my white bead slipped off my needle. Hank bolted to the couch, a small reindeer clutched in his hand, and deposited his ass beside mine.

"Move over." Becky arrived a moment later and wiggled between us. "I want to see Tyr make sport, too."

"Don't you be making doe eyes at my man now," I teased. Becky giggled. Hank shushed us both. I rolled my eyes. Who cared about the anthem? All I wanted to see was—"Tyr!" I squealed as the camera panned down a line of incredibly sexy men rocking back and forth in the bench pen area thingy. "He looks good in red," I sighed, then fanned myself with my muff. Rabbit hair filled the air. Hmm. "Does a muff shed?"

"I'm always spitting out hair," Hank commented. Becky slapped his arm. I giggled at the two of them. Such a cute couple. Were Tyr and I cute? I had to assume so. He was so rugged and manly, and I was simply adorable. Of course, we were cute!

"Are the Mules good?" Becky asked. Hank nodded. I returned to my beading. The men on the TV were making a goalie comparison. As the play-by-play man and the color man gabbled on about goals against numbers, I attached another pearly bead to my muff.

The puck drop took place as I threaded my needle. I scanned the players on the ice and didn't see Tyr, so I went back to work. I only had five days to complete this ensemble. I had a short week at the Campo, then I was off to New York for the Miss Gay NY City pageant on the twenty-fourth. After that, I had the Femme Gay Southern pageant at the Glass Hat Saloon in Charlotte, North Carolina on New Year's Eve. My booking agenda was packed. Which was a good thing, but it curtailed time with Tyr tremendously.

"Why are they just skating up and down on the ice? Where is Tyr?" I asked when I glanced at the game.

"It's hockey. They're supposed to skate up and down on the ice." I threw my brother a dark look. "Tyr's on the fourth line. Didn't you see the line-ups as they scrolled over the screen?"

"Hello? Muff?!" I waved it around and more fur filled the air. "I think it has mange. Can a muff have mange?"

"It's not real rabbit," Hank sniped.

"Gasp! You take that back! Gigi Patel LeBay only wears

real furs, you monster!" I flicked a bead at his head. Becky laughed at the bead-to-nose impact. Hank was not amused.

"There, Tyr is coming out on the ice now." Hank pointed at the screen. Oh my yes, he was a sexy beast. All that hair and muscle. Well, the muscle was hidden at the moment, but I knew it was there. I was intimately familiar with all his bulges. I'd tongued each inch of his yummy body. Every nook and cranny had been—

"Oh, look at him go! Boo on the white team. Stop stealing the puck from my man! Oh! He got it back! Look at him go. He's incredibly fast for such a burly man. Shoot the puck! Okay, he shot. He listens to me! He did quite well. Did you see him shooting?"

"Yep, he shot the puck. Quality chance there." Hank grinned at me.

I preened, beaded, yelled, and nearly fainted when Tyr was knocked off his skates by a gorilla in a white jersey. I chewed on my lip until Tyr got up and skated down the ice. Thank God. Becky made popcorn. We snacked and rooted on my man. After a while, it got kind of boring.

"Why do they just skate up and down the ice?" I asked again, because nothing was happening, and I was growing bored. Like beading, only with less to show for it.

"What do you want them to do? Cartwheels?" Hank asked around a mouthful of cheddar cheese popcorn.

"I want them to make me pee my pants. Why isn't Tyr out there more? He's clearly the best player on the team. Oh! There he is. Oh, yummy. He's so cute. Is he allowed to do that? Wait. Why did he get sent to hockey prison? That big dolt obviously stepped on Tyr's stick. Tripping?! Oh, please, go buy some bifocals, referee man! I hate this game.

Turn it off. *No!* Don't you dare. Tyr said he was going to score a goal for me."

"It's like watching hockey with a three-year-old," Hank mumbled to Becky then ducked another incoming bead.

"I'm right here, bitch," I snapped, then something big happened on the TV. I wasn't sure what started it, as I'd been flicking beads at my brother, but suddenly, one of the announcers was yelling loudly. "Oh! What's happening?!"

"Oh, shit, Tyr's on a breakaway! Did you see that blind backhanded pass from Bedard!?" Hank shot to his sock-covered feet; eyes glued to the screen.

"A what? I know what a backhanded compliment is. Oh, shit! My little lamb has the puck! Look at him go! Shoot the puck! Shoot the puck!" Tyr did shoot as if he had heard my shouts. The puck disappeared between the goalie's legs, then reappeared behind him in the net. Tyr kissed two fingers then lifted them into the air. An homage to his father, I assumed. Then, all the men in red jerseys jumped on him. I leapt up onto the sofa, shouting and clapping and yes, crying, as Tyr smiled at his new teammates.

"Dude needs to tighten up his five hole," Hank shouted over the TV.

"I hate floppy five holes!" I replied, then continued jumping. My brother roared. Hank and Becky joined me on the sofa where we had a bounce fest, until one of the couch legs broke off. Giggling and out of breath, we shoved a few books under one end of the couch then flopped down again, eyes riveted to the game. For a little bit, anyway. The second and third periods weren't very exciting, to be honest. Tyr didn't score again but he did crunch several men. The Mules won by that single goal that my man had scored. Big men in too tight suits after the game raved about Tyr for a few moments. They then moved onto some other big news hockey sport story about some player on another team looking to leave that team. Hank was interested, but I could care less. If Tyr wasn't making hockey or being talked about, it was blah to me.

"Where are you going?" Hank asked after Becky dragged him to the tree by his ear.

"I have rehearsal for the holiday show," I reminded him.

"Fill up the truck before you bring it home." He tossed me his keys. I promised I would, then gathered up my beads and muff, dropped them off in my sewing room, and then hurried to pull on some tights, a bright pink oversized shirt, and some heels. I pulled on a lime green coat that I'd found at the thrift shop, then pulled a yellow toque down over my head. I sighed at my pale face in the mirror. I did need some makeup, but I was breaking out, so today I'd declared a clean face day. Hopefully, none of the bitches at work would comment.

OF COURSE, the bitches at work commented.

One bitch commented, I should say, and it was fine because her saltiness was just adding to the smack down she was about to incur.

"Maybe you should try a little astringent to help clean out those huge pores of yours," Monique threw at me as I trudged to the stage. Why, by all the motherfucking gods of drag, was this bitch always on stage with me? I was going to have to speak to Mother. It was obvious the harpy had no talent. All she had was face, and that was starting to show signs of wear. Did she have body? Meh. Maybe if you squinted and missed her back rolls. It was like a can of Pillsbury dough hanging over the top of her corset.

"Maybe you should try stuffing those crescent rolls down into your corset," I snapped back as I climbed onstage. Clarice was seated at a table, making her newly crowned managerial position known to one and all. Sitka was seated with her, both were poring over paperwork of some sort while Monique, Jo-Jo, and a part-timer named Alabaster—just Alabaster—was working on her tuck. Why the bitch was tucked for a rehearsal, I didn't know. But the tuck was a little meaty, so work away! "While I have you here, I need to discuss that backstabbing shit you pulled with my man."

Cord walked past the stage with a crate of whiskey. He paused. Sitka and Clarice looked up from the books.

"As if I would backstab you for that ugly ape," Monique replied as she fiddled with the new orange wig she had demanded she wear for our group number. Orange. For a Christmas show. The whore had no taste. And she was about to be missing a few teeth.

"Oh please, you fucking *wish* you were getting some of what I'm getting."

"Ladies," Sitka growled.

"And what are you getting, other than left behind while he moves to greener and far less acne-filled pastures," Monique fired back as I stalked toward her. Jo-Jo and Alabaster both began slowly inching away exit stage left.

The bitch. How dare she talk about my face? "You know what the hell I'm talking about. You told Tyr that I was done with him. You tried to sabotage my relationship. I am going to pound you into the floor, you scaggy cow!"

"That would be the only pounding you've *ever* done," Monique countered.

"*Ladies*," Sitka warned.

"Accurate, but irrelevant," I snarled, then took a swing.

It probably looked nothing like Tyr when he was fighting, but it did land on the side of her fat head. Monique yelped and hit me in the face, her fist finding my right eye. It hurt like a motherfucker, but I was too pissed off to care. I ripped her wig off. She slapped me across the face. I jumped on her, sending her careening around the stage, flailing at me as I cuffed her. Queens were screaming and cussing and running and wailing. Someone pulled me off Monique's back. I spat and clawed like a cat as Cord carted me off the stage. My one heel fell off. Sitka had an arm around Monique's flabby middle and Clarice was trying to calm down Jo-Jo and Alabaster, who were both crying while flapping about the club like hysterical nellies.

I was unceremoniously deposited in a bar stool. "Sit there. Do not move!" Cord waved a finger at me, then scooted behind the bar to fill a white bar towel with ice. "Here, put this on that eye."

I winced when I applied the ice pack to my weepy eye. Monique and Sitka were having a royal bitch fest behind me. I was only half listening, because now that the adrenaline spike of my first ever fight was waning, my eye was hurting more and more.

"I think it's going to be a shiner," Cord tenderly said, then pushed a glass of Sprite at me. "Tyr will be so proud. He's dating a Valkyrie."

"Hell, yeah," I groaned, envisioning the black eye that

I'd have to perform with. I sipped at the lemon-lime soda, then swallowed down some aspirin that Clarice brought me. She sat down on my left, rubbing my back as I whimpered over my shiner. Was it shining already? What the hell had I been thinking? I had shows to do, pageants to win.

Still, bitch, you are a fucking Valkyrie.

Yeah, I was. Sitka stormed past, dragging Monique along by her corset strings. I shot a look at Jo-Jo and Alabaster, who were still hiding in the wings. We all were deadly quiet as Mother tossed her child out onto the cold sidewalk in only a corset, fishnets, and tacky heels.

"Bye, Felicia!" I yelled at the top of my lungs. "Don't forget her ugly wig," I called out as Sitka stalked back to the bar. I got a dark, dark look, then a kiss on the forehead from my drag mother.

"You're a violent bitch," Sitka sighed as she hauled her tall frame up into a stool. "Miserable cow. It was past time someone slapped her upside her hollow head."

"I feel bad, now," I moaned. Mother looked at me. "What? I do!" Her sculpted eyebrows knitted in disbelief. "Okay, fine, I don't feel bad. I'm glad you showed her to the door. She was a busted-up sow."

"No one comes at me with a washed-up bar queen comment and continues to flounce her pussy on *my* stage," Sitka growled. "Give me a cocktail. Jesus Christ. It's not even six pm yet. You bitches make me drink."

"Right, like it's us that did that," Clarice slipped in as Cord made us all cocktails. Jo-Jo and Alabaster—whose boy name escaped me at the moment, because my eyeball was tearing and turning black—slowly emerged from the sidelines. Vodka and cranberry were too tempting to pass up.

Mother waved that comment off. "Cord, go find Eladio and have him pack up Monique's shit. Place it outside the backdoor. She can pick up her trash by the dumpster like the dusty bitch she is."

We all snapped our fingers in agreement. "Now for you. The next time you throw a fist in my club, I will dock your pay and take your best wig." I gasped. "Was it worth it?"

I took a sip of my cocktail. Fuck, but my eye hurt. "Was what worth it?"

"Getting clocked in the mug. Was it worth it? Is *he* worth it?" Mother asked but all ears were tuned to my reply.

"He's totally worth it."

"Hmmm." That was all Mother Sitka said, but the others slid in to give me hugs and whispers of thanks for standing up to a bitch.

I'd do it all over again. No bitch comes between me and my lambkins. The only thing that might break us up was distance, but I would go down swinging. I'd keep sneaking around for the next twenty years if I had to. I'd hate it, but I'd do it. I loved him. It was just that simple.

AN HOUR LATER, I was in the dressing room, pouting over my rapidly purpling eye socket. I'd have to use a damn spatula to get enough base, foundation, and concealer on to hide this monstrosity. Still totally worth it. My phone buzzed. I blew off some dusting powder that had settled

on it when Jo-Jo had to grab an extra shift because
Monique was now serving waffles or something. I saw it
was my Viking and hurried to take the call.

Tyr's handsome face appeared. His eyebrows shot up
his forehead. I pushed my lower lip out.

"What happened to you?" he asked, his voice soft with
concern.

"I got into a fight." His jaw dropped. "Seriously. I
punched Monique in the face for trying to dick with us.
Then, Mother threw her out into the cold for calling her a
bar queen."

"But, she owns a bar, so…"

"Oh, you sweet summer child." I sighed as my gaze
moved from him to my face. "Bar queen is not nice. So
yeah, ding-dong, the bitch is dead. Which old bitch? That
doughy bitch!"

"You're wicked."

"Ah, ha, I see what you did there. So, my face is purple
and hurts. I wish you were here to kiss it better. I don't
think I'll be able to make the New York pageant with my
face like this."

"I wish I was there, too. So, did you really get into a
fight?"

"Why do you doubt?"

"Because you're so against violence."

"Oh. Well, yes, that's true. But the whore had it
coming."

"I see."

"Don't judge. It's unbecoming. I saw you score for
me!" He smiled that shy smile of his that made my belly
turn to jelly. "I watched the whole game and only
complained about being bored ten or eleven times. Ignore

Hank if he says otherwise." I placed my icy towel back on my swelling eye.

"I'm glad you enjoyed it." He seemed off somehow. As if he were running at only seventy percent instead of a full battery. "I'm back at the hotel now and it's nice and all but…"

"But you wish you had a drag queen there with you."

"Yes, do you know any?"

"Shady bitch." He chuckled wistfully. The poor lamb. I wished we could align a time to see each other, but our travel schedules were too busy. "I wish you were here. Or I was there. I'm not going to handle this long-distance relationship well. I'm going to be a whiny Wanda."

"Me, too. It's funny." He removed his beret then sat down. I longed to climb into his lap. "Tonight was exciting and all. The realization of a dream. I'm just not sure if it's my dream that became a reality today or my father's."

I stared into his acorn-colored eyes. "You'll figure it out."

He shrugged. We talked about other things. Tried to plan for a visit over Christmas, but he only had one day off and had to be on a plane for some Canadian city ridiculously early the day after Christmas. Me going to him was out, as Hank and Becky were driving to her parents for another holiday filled with cranberry salad and upper-class displeasure. Sadness crept into the call and he signed off shortly after our failed attempts to meet up.

"I need some sleep. I'm exhausted." He looked done in. "I love you. Somehow, we'll make this work. I promise and you know I always keep my promises."

"I know, lamb, I know."

I blew him several goodbye kisses. He whispered

lovely soft things in Danish, then ended the call. Feeling down now, I moved my make-up case to the empty place that Monique's departure had left behind. Now that she was gone, I was happy to be back here with my sisters. If only my relationship woes were as easy to handle as a bag of blush, wig glue, and false eyelashes.

Chapter Seventeen

TYR

I'd played three games in Chicago.

I'd gotten a goal, an assist, and five hits. Oh, and blocked a shot that had left a welted bruise on my left calf that was the size of a grapefruit. December twenty-fourth, the head coach of the Mules called me into his office to thank me for my contributions, but my services were no longer needed.

It didn't truly surprise me. I'd been in this game long enough to know that minor league players were constantly being shuffled to the pros then sent back down. Timothy Klick, a defenseman on the Warthogs who had retired last year, had made the trip to Chicago fourteen times in his career. The longest he had stayed was two months.

"But I thought Morgan had a concussion," I said while Coach Pendergrass divvied his attention between me and game tapes on his tablet.

"He does, but Montgomery is back, so we're just going to shuffle Benson and Levesque around a bit. It's only a light concussion so Morgan is pretty much day to day. You did good, Hemmingsen. Keep that fire lit and maybe next time we see you, you'll stay around longer."

He shook my hand. I thanked him and left, stopping in the locker room to gather my personal effects—there weren't many because I'd had a feeling my stay might not be long—and said goodbye to a few of the guys.

When I stepped out into the brutal cold of a Chicago morning, I glanced skyward. There was snow predicted for Christmas day, but not until late. With a nasty biting wind whirling around me, I turned my back to the gust and checked my phone. If I got a rental car lined up through the team, I could be home by midnight. In my six and a half days away from Wilmington, I had made some decisions. Big ones that had the potential to shake up not only my life, but the Warthogs. Even so, with that possibility looming over me, I felt freer now than I had ever felt before. Odd that a man who should be devastated by being shipped back to the minors was actually happy to go.

Shivering a bit, I called Jimmy for a ride. Within five minutes, a car pulled up that whisked me to my hotel. I packed up. It didn't take long. Then, I was taken to the airport, where I rented a commonsense sort of vehicle. An SUV with four-wheel drive, in case I ran into bad weather. The team was picking up the bill, so I got the fanciest SUV they had on the lot. It was like riding on a cloud. While I waited in the car rental lobby for them to gas up the dark green SUV, I sent out a request to the Warthogs in our team chat. I knew they'd be on the ice now; they were playing a home game against Scranton at noon. Then, I composed a message for my head coach. It was a short one, basically telling him that I was gay and wished to speak to him tomorrow morning about my future with the team. Once that was sent, I slid behind the wheel at ten after twelve, found the Bluetooth setting, and linked my phone to the stereo system.

Eli had made me a playlist so that I'd not forget him while I was gone. Not that I would ever forget the man who had rescued me from a life of chains. The first song came on and I smiled. It was one of the songs he performed on stage as Gigi. If I closed my eyes, I could see him on stage in a slinky gown. If I breathed in deeply, the faintest scent of rose caressed my senses. If only I could touch him.

Soon. Soon, you'll be able to hold your heart's desire.

I glanced into the backseat to double check. Yes, my bags and laptop case were there. I did *not* want to leave my laptop behind. I'd created something for Eli on it. Something that I felt was magnificent, but he might scoff at. Hell, the world might scoff at it. That was a chance I was going to have to take. My future held lots of possible landmines. All I could do now was move through the minefield with as much care as I could muster and pray I stepped properly.

"Watch over me, Mama," I whispered, leaving my father's dream for me in that cold, windy city by the mighty lake.

I ARRIVED in Wilmington at a few minutes past 11:30 pm on Christmas Eve. I sped to Campo Royale, ignoring all the buzzing and shimmying that my phone had been doing for hours. I didn't dare reply to anyone. I had this plan, and I was going to see it through. The chips, then, would fall where they may.

The flashing red lips on the wet street set off a cascade of joy mixed with terror in my breast. Slipping into a parking slot down the street, I locked the doors, shoved my fob into the front pocket of my jeans, and stepped out into a cold drizzle. Marcus the doorman waved me in, setting off some sour looks from the damp patrons who were in line.

I apologized over my shoulder to the angry people, then ducked inside, my heart thumping, sending blood coursing through my ears, dulling the grating monotone of Sitka announcing the final act of the evening. I removed my beret, ran my fingers through my hair, and forged onward. Parting the crowd around the bar, I made eye contact with Dante, Maya, Ben, and several other Warthogs. Dante and Ben looked utterly confused when I nudged my way past them. Gigi had just taken the stage. My sight was locked on the beautiful platinum blonde wearing a cute little holiday dress. Ben said something, but I zoned it out. I'd deal with him, and all the rest after I did what I had to do.

"Good evening," Gigi said with a smile for the happy crowd. "I'm going to leap right into things with a snappy number from Patti Page called 'Boogie Woogie Santa' that will get your toes tapping and your—"

Her witty dialog died off when she saw me coming closer. She threw her hands up to cover the lower half of her face while her music began. I climbed up on the stage,

Gigi's perfectly lined eyes growing wider and wider with each passing second. We stood facing each other as a soft white spotlight lingered on us.

"I'm home," I said, the microphone picking up my words. Hell, it was probably picking up the pounding of my heart. How could it not be? It was deafening. "I mean that in every possible way. This town is my home, this club and all the welcoming, accepting people who come here are my home, and you're my home."

"Oh my God, what are you *doing*?!" Gigi squeaked as tears welled in her bittersweet chocolate eyes.

"I'm telling the world that I'm gay. And that you're my boyfriend. And that I love you and want to spend the rest of my life with you at my side."

The background music stopped. Perhaps time even stopped. Not a noise was made in that club. No one said a damn thing, until Gigi squealed and threw herself at me. Her mouth found mine. I lifted her from the stage, hands cradling her ass, and I kissed her with all the fire, passion, and love that I'd kept bottled up inside of me for years. She linked her ankles behind my ass, her long nails raking over my scalp.

"I love you too, lamb. So much!" Gigi whispered when we came up for breath. That was when the crowd leapt to its feet to cheer. My cheeks burned, but I claimed another taste of my boyfriend's sweet mouth. "I want to go home now. Right now. I need you inside me."

The crowd cheered even louder. My face flamed at the rowdy and lewd calls, but I pushed through the embarrassment. Carrying my man off the stage, I skidded to a halt when Sitka stepped in front of us, her arms folded over a dress with a black velvet top, a wide red sash, and a skirt that was covered with reindeer.

"If you make my daughter cry one more time, I will come after you with the fury of a menopausal badger suffering with a raging yeast infection. Understand, Kitty Boy?"

"Yes, Mother," I said as Gigi hung off me like a lemur, covering my face with lipstick marks as the crowd cheered and pointed us toward the front door.

"Go, then. I'll finish the show. But don't make a habit of this," Sitka told Gigi.

"Yes, Mother. I love you!" The tiny queen in my arms shouted at her drag mother while Sitka made her way to the stage.

Sitka flipped us the bird. I kissed Gigi again, then met the questioning eyes of my teammates. Well, not all of them were questioning. Dante was grinning madly.

"About damn time!" he shouted over the licentious hoots and hollers filling the Campo. I inclined my head. Ben stood there, shellshocked. The other Warthogs were clapping, but not Ben. Tough titties, as Sitka was known to say. He could accept the gay player on the team, or he could fuck off. I was done hiding. The chains were officially snapped, and I was not going to allow myself to be shackled ever again. I carried Gigi out the front door to wild applause. She was mouthing my neck and jaw, making it hard to walk. We took a short make-out break outside the club.

"Home…now…you big brave Viking, you," Gigi panted beside my ear. I turned to carry her to the car when someone called my name. I tensed, placed Gigi to the sidewalk with care, and then slowly moved to face Ben.

"If you're going to say something stupid or insulting to me or my boyfriend, I'd strongly suggest you don't." It was no idle threat. I'd cleaned his clock once. I would do it again. No one talked shit about Eli.

He raised both hands. "No, I would never." I cocked an eyebrow. Gigi snorted as I stepped in front of her. He glanced away, then dragged his gaze back to mine. "Okay, I deserve that. I didn't know you were...you know. *Gay*. If I had, I wouldn't have said the things I did."

"You would have thought them, though," Gigi tossed over my shoulder, her slim form tight to my back.

He opened his mouth to retaliate, then exhaled. When his lungs were empty, he nodded.

"Yeah, I would have thought it. I was raised—" He paused to check himself. "No, I'm not going to make excuses. I'd like to say that I'm sorry. I've learned a lot in those diversity programs, and I wanted to apologize. I'm trying." I folded my arms over my chest and leveled an icy look at him. "Okay, I deserved that as well. I *am* trying. I will try harder. I didn't know. I like you, Tyr. I just never would have suspected that someone as..." He pressed his lips tightly closed. "Forget that, too. Just..." His shoulders sagged. "Just know that I'm trying to better myself. Leave that shit behind that my father used to say. You know how it is with sons and fathers, right?"

I did know. And so, I gave him another chance. Sometimes, it took people time to divest themselves of the shit drummed into them as children.

With a nod, I offered him my hand. He gave me a wobbly smile as he pumped my hand. Just once. And he never moved to shake or make apologies to Eli. But it was a start. Maybe, when we all returned to the barn after the holidays, we could start working on being a team again. They would have to learn to accept, and I would have to trust. We'd all have to work on rebuilding faith in each other.

"Thanks. And uhm…nice dress, Gigi." Ben backed up, then shuffled down the sidewalk, hands in the front pockets of his winter coat.

"Can we go screw like wild ferrets now?" I chuckled then gathered my man up, sweeping him off his tiny heels, and jogging to the rental. I was so glad I'd taken a contract for three days.

How I ever managed to drive to Gigi's place and not wreck, I do not know. The gods were truly watching over us. My boyfriend was feeling me up the entire ride home. By the time I got himinto his house ,my cock was so hard it ached like a broken bone. I began tugging at his clothing.

"Easy, easy. One does not manhandle an adorable little vintage dress like this," she panted as I worked on the tiny buttons on the back of her holiday dress. "God, okay, stop. Let me. Wait…ugh, fucking buttons."

I lifted the skirt with the candy canes up over her head, pulling the dress and her wig off in one tug. Buttons did hit the floor. Eli groaned at the sound, but then climbed up over me as if I were a jungle gym. The Christmas tree winked and blinked as we stripped bare then feasted on each other. We fumbled and fell over each other, tasting and touching and laughing, as we bumbled into his bedroom. He gave me a shove that sent me to my back on his bed.

"I need to take my face off," he said, but jumped on

me, lining his cock up next to mine. "I want you to know that you're fucking Eli."

"I know who I'm making love to. The man that captured my heart. Never any question." He bit down on his puffy lip, whimpered, and then claimed my mouth. I eased him upward, my cock leaving a wet streak along his taint.

"You are a sweet, dear lamb," he choked out, cradling my face as he licked into my mouth. The kisses grew hotter, wetter, deeper. We were frantic. He was slicking up my cock then his hole, his lithe body undulating as he worked lube into his ass. "Love me."

"Always. I will always love you. Eli...*shit!*" He eased down onto me, his heat swallowing me up, then hugging my prick. I arched up. He tossed his head this way and that, blue hair sticking to smeared makeup.

His body was made for mine. It enveloped me. Words fell by the wayside as he rose and fell, his ass slapping my thighs as he propelled us to climaxes that wrung us out. His cock spurted violently, coating my belly with spunk. My dick kicked madly. I held him tight, my grip unforgiving as I pumped and thrust, rolling us over so I could drive deeper. Eli cooed and whispered sweet little things. Silly nothings that encouraged me to go deeper, harder.

We lay there afterward, lost in the glow of our love, our bodies trembling and damp, twined together like climbing roses. The scent of that flower filled my soul. I breathed him in, kissed a path to his smooth armpit, then back to his tempting mouth.

"I love you so much," he crooned as I eased out of him.

I wiped him off with a shirt that had been tossed to the floor. He lay there, splayed out, eyes burning with emotion, body pinked from sex, and let me tidy him up. The man was terribly spoiled. "That was the craziest thing I have ever seen a man do," he said when I tossed the soiled shirt to the hamper in the corner. "You've probably detonated your hockey career."

"I don't care." I threw the covers up over him. "I have something to show you."

"Oh, sakes, you already showed me that, big boy," he said in a perfect Mae West impersonation. What did it say about me that I now knew who Mae West, Judy Garland, The Andrew Sisters, and Liza Minelli were? It said that my life had changed in dramatic ways. "I bet you will care when the shit hits the fan tomorrow."

"I don't. I mean…okay, yes, I do in one way. But in another, I don't. The hockey culture was choking the life out of me. If they can't accept a gay player with a drag queen boyfriend on the team, then I'm happy to quit. I have other things in my life now." He didn't appear convinced. "Wait here."

I leaped from the bed, pulled on my jeans, and darted out of the room. Eli was calling after me as I jogged to the front door then barreled outside. The sidewalk and lawn were bitter cold. I hopped and skipped to my rental, grabbed my bags, and then ran right back to Eli. He screamed when I dove under the covers, then pulled his toasty warm body to my icy one.

"You are a certifiable madman!" He giggled and playfully slapped as I peeled off my jeans under the covers. "What the hell was that important that you had to leave my bed for? Has the bloom gone off the rose already?"

"Hush." I kissed the pout from his pink lips then hoisted my laptop bag up into bed with us. "When I was in Chicago, I made a lot of decisions."

"Obviously. Seems you could have shared about the one you just sprang on me and half your teammates." He snuggled up close as my laptop slowly warmed up.

"I didn't feel like regurgitating the same story a few dozen times. A sharp cut hurts less than a dull one. Now it's done. They know. The team knows. They can do as they all wish."

"Madman," he sighed as he wiped at his face with a tissue. "I need to take this off. My skin is already—uhm, okay, what are we doing here? Are you showing me porn?!"

"No. Not porn. A possible future if hockey turns against me. And a gift for my beautiful boyfriend." I placed the laptop in front of him. He gave me a suspicious look but lifted the Dell from the bed to his thighs. My phone buzzed from the floor. I was tempted to ignore it, but Eli gave me that look of his, so I fished around inside my pants and found my cell. It was a lone text from the Warthogs owner.

"Guess this is it," I mumbled. Eli looked up. "It's the owner, Myron McMillian."

"Oh, dear. Best read it. Sharp cuts and all." He closed the laptop.

The text was short, succinct, and to the point.

The Warthogs are an inclusive team and organization. I expect to see you on the ice in two days. Merry Christmas. ~ Myron McMillian

"I think it might be okay?" I showed him the text.

"Oh, yes, that's a very okay text! Reply to him. Tell him that you want a special seat for your fabulous boyfriend right behind home plate."

"Shady bitch," I muttered, then leaned in to kiss his bare shoulder.

"Listen to you, learning the lingo!" He smiled softly then reopened the laptop. I sent Myron a short reply, thanking him for being so openminded and saying I would be at morning skate on Friday. What I'd run into when I showed up, I didn't know, but with the team behind me, I felt as if it would be okay. Eventually. Once the hysteria about the War God of Wilmington being gay died down. "Back to my gift!" His eyes rounded as he skimmed. "Oh, my gods, it's my fairy tale!" He flung his dirty tissue to the side then hunched over the laptop. "Listen to this! 'Once upon a time, there was a fabulous prince who enchanted all the lads in the kingdom with his beautiful voice and eye for courtly fashion.'" His gaze darted to me. "Did you hear that?!"

"I wrote it."

"Oh. Well, sure. Of course you did, but it's amazing! Where do you come in?"

"I'm the cassowary." I slid an arm around him and eased him into my side, the laptop coming to rest on my stomach.

"Oh! Do I get to kiss you and break the curse upon your lonely heart?"

"You do. Just like you did in real life."

The End

Coming next in the Campo Royale series...

The Bachelor and the Cherry (Campo Royale #2)

JORDAN STEVENS HAS CRAMMED a lot of living into his fifty years. Some of those years have been good, some bad, and some he would just as soon forget. The world isn't always kind to an aging queen. Lovers begin to scamper into forbidden fields, your padding tends to slip, and you spend more time with egg whites than most pastry chefs. Heartache is nothing new to the man who embodies the acid-tongued Sitka Patel on stage every night, which led Jordan to vow to never trust another man under eighty again. He has his club, his drag family, and his Siamese cat Heckle. Who needs the hassle? That philosophy had served him well, until a stunning young thing with dark chocolate eyes shows up at the back door of Campo Royale with a suitcase, a sad story, and a dream.

FROM THE TIME he was old enough to spell the word sequin, Yampier Perez knew that someday he'd be wearing them. The youngest of four children born to Cuban immigrants, Yampier was always a little glitzier than the other neighborhood boys. His love of fashion design and performance arts was barely tolerated at home and even less so in the hallways of his rural Georgia high school. Yet, Yampier never let his light be doused, not even the day his older brother caught him modeling his sister's prom dress. Beaten, disowned, and on his own before graduation, he found himself having to work seedy jobs doing even seedier things, until he saved enough cash to head to the Big Apple. That money has now run out, leaving him stuck in Wilmington with no food, no place to stay, and no family. Little does he know that stumbling into the Campo Royale Club, half frozen and weak from hunger, is about to bring him everything he has yearned for: Acceptance, a spotlight, and the love of a kindhearted —if somewhat acerbic—older man.

A note from the author…

If you enjoyed *The Viking and the Drag Queen (Campo Royale #1)*, I'd be incredibly grateful if you could leave a review on a major retailer site, BookBub, Goodreads, or on your personal social media platforms.

Reviews are the reason someone else might decide to give this book a try!

Deepest thanks,

squishy hugs

V.L.

Have you read?

Have you read Dawn's Desire - book one in the new Prairie Smoke Ranch trilogy.

Read Dawn's Desire

Amid fossils, yarrow, and cattle, two men are about to discover a love bigger than the Wyoming sky.

When Nate Pearson left heartache behind in the big city, he never looked back, he couldn't bear to. Suffering and loss propelled him westward, but once he laid eyes on the Tetons, he knew he'd found a place where he could hide and heal. For over twenty years, the Prairie Smoke Ranch has been his refuge and his salvation. Working under the pale blue sky, he's been able to keep the pain buried. Then one day while digging a cattle watering system, Nate and his hands unearth a mound of dinosaur bones that will change his life forever.

Once news of the discovery reaches the local university, paleontology professor Bishop Haney arrives with several undergrads to spend the summer excavating and cataloging the find. At first, Nate is unimpressed with the laid-back, surfer dude with the ocean blue eyes. But as the two opposites get to know each other, Nate discovers Bishop might be the balm his aching soul needs.

Read Dawn's Desire

———————

Dawn's Desire | Twilight's Touch *(coming February 11, 2022)* | Dusk's Devotion *(coming June 17, 2022)*

A note from VL Locey

If you enjoyed *The Viking and the Drag Queen*, I'd be incredibly grateful if you could leave a review on a major retailer site, BookBub, Goodreads, or on your personal social media platforms.

Reviews are the reason someone else might decide to give this book a try!
Deepest thanks,
squishy hugs

V.L.

Also by V.L. Locey

Colors of Love Series

Lost in Indigo | Touch of a Yellow Sun | The Good Green Earth | Slow Dances Under an Orange Moon | A Brush of Blue | Songs of Red Currant Wine | Pines & Violets

According to Liam Series

Life According to Liam | Christmas According to Liam | Love According to Liam | World According to Liam | Family According to Liam

Prairie Smoke Ranch series

Dawn's Desire | Twilight's Touch *(coming February 11, 2022)* | Dusk's Devotion *(coming June 17, 2022)*

Campo Royale

The Viking and the Drag Queen *(Coming Jan. 5, 2022)* | The Bachelor and the Cherry *(Coming April 20,2022* | The Barkeep and the Bookseller *(Coming August 5, 2022)* | *The Financier and the Sweetheart (Coming 2023)* | *The Chanteuse and the Soldier (Coming 2023)*

Tales of Bryant

Tales of Bryant | Nine Small Sips | Fade In | Reserved |
Safflower | Curtain Call

Cayuga Cougars Series

Snap Shot | Open Net | Coach's Challenge | Overtime | One-
on-One | A Star-Crossed Christmas *(A Cayuga Cougars Short)*

Point Shot Trilogy Boxed Set *(including Two Man Advantage, Game
Misconduct, and Full Strength)*

Overtime – The Trilogy

Rebound | Final Shot | Draw

Laurel Holidays

The Christmas Oaks | The Christmas Pundit | The Christmas
Tenor *(Coming December 2021)* | The Christmas Rescue *(Coming
November 18, 2022)*

Erie

An Erie Collection

Nightside—An Erie Vampire Tale

Gems

The Gems Collection (including Opal, Garnet, Diamond, & Onyx

Standalone Stories

Holly & Hockey Boots | Life is a Stevie Wonder Song | Blue Line Collection #1 | Improper Fraction | Love is a Walk in the Park | Shake the Stars | Loving Layne | The New York Nightwings Collection | Love of the Hunter | The Ballad of Crow and Sparrow | Bayte & Tackle *(Coming October 7, 2022)*

Written with RJ Scott

Harrisburg Railers (Hockey Romance)

Changing Lines | First Season | Deep Edge | Poke Check | Last Defense | Goal Line | Neutral Zone | Hat Trick | Save The Date | Baby Makes Three

Railers Volume 1 | Railers Volume 2 | Railers Volume 3

Owatonna U Hockey (Hockey Romance)

Ryker | Scott | Benoit | Christmas Lights | Valentine's Hearts | Desert Dreams

Arizona Raptors (Hockey Romance)

Coast To Coast | Across the Pond | Shadow and Light | Sugar and Ice | School and Rock

Boston Rebels (Hockey Romance)

Top Shelf | Back Check | Snowed

To Love a Wildcat Series

Pink Pucks & Power Plays (*To Love a Wildcat #1*)

A Most Unlikely Countess (*To Love a Wildcat #2*)

O Captain! My Captain! (*To Love a Wildcat #3*)

Reality Check (*To Love a Wildcat #4*)

Language of Love (*To Love a Wildcat #5*)

Final Shifts (*To Love a Wildcat #6*)

Meet V.L. Locey

V.L. Locey loves worn jeans, yoga, belly laughs, walking, reading and writing lusty tales, Greek mythology, the New York Rangers, comic books, and coffee.

(Not necessarily in that order.)

She shares her life with her husband, her daughter, one dog, two cats, a flock of assorted domestic fowl, and two Jersey steers.

When not writing spicy romances, she enjoys spending her day with her menagerie in the rolling hills of Pennsylvania with a cup of fresh java in hand.

vllocey.com
vicki@vllocey.com

Newsletter - vllocey.com/newsletter

facebook.com/V.L.Locey
twitter.com/vllocey
instagram.com/vl_locey
bookbub.com/authors/v-l-locey
goodreads.com/vllocey
pinterest.com/vllocey

Made in United States
North Haven, CT
06 January 2022

14255030R10137